NYX

Loren Walker

Octopus & Elephant Books
PROVIDENCE, RHODE ISLAND

Octopus & Elephant Books
www.oandebooks.com

Publisher's Note: This is a work of fiction. Names, characters, places, and incidents are a product of the author's imagination. Any resemblance to actual people, living or dead, or to businesses, companies, events, institutions, or locales is completely coincidental.

Book Layout ©2015 BookDesignTemplates.com.

Cover by Deranged Doctor Designs.

INSYNN / Loren Walker. -- 1st ed.
ISBN 978-0-9973922-7-2

Contents

For the ones that I love.

PART ONE

Renzo's head hit the floor with a crack. Cohen stumbled over his feet, his back slamming against the wall before his body slid down. Phaira clawed at something invisible, before letting out a pained sigh and collapsing. Sydel's fall was grace-ful, though, like a dancer at the end of a performance, CaLarca couldn't help but notice, even as she used every ounce of her Eko to render the girl unconscious.

It wouldn't last long, CaLarca reminded herself, a headache pounding through her skull, her lungs breathless from the ef-fort. *You must move.*

It took the rest of CaLarca's strength, and her SCKAFO leg braces cranked up to maximum support, to drag the four bodies through the *Arazura.* First, Renzo: her arms looped around his chest; the sound of his feet, one metal, one flesh, quietly bang-ing down the stairs, as she took one careful step at a time. She could see the pink burns on his arms, on the back of his neck; remnants from the battle a week ago. She gave a silent apology and laid him in the grass.

Cohen was so huge and heavy that any way to push him for-ward was acceptable. With a final heave, he tumbled through the exit and landed in a heap. She didn't care. He'd always been cruel to her; if he woke bruised, so be it. She had the same bit-ter impulse with Phaira, but wariness overtook her disdain, so instead she set the woman down carefully next to her broth-ers. Sydel was the lightest of the four, the easiest to hoist over her shoulder. Being so physically close to all of them made her uncomfortable: the smell of them, their skin already puckering from the cold wind.

When it was done, CaLarca studied the four silhouettes. Then, kneeling down in the mud, she placed Phaira's katana blade, sheathed in its black case, on the ground. Better than a handgun, to stay off patrol radar. And now they could defend themselves, if necessary. The Byrne siblings were resourceful. Sydel was morally strong. They would understand why she did this, eventually. They would likely come after her, but hopefully she had time to confirm what she longed to be true since the day she heard about the burned bodies.

Her husband and son were alive.

And they were waiting for her.

Still, it was a relief to seal the entryway with a spin of the wheel, and make her way to the cockpit. The *Arazura* was eerily silent: no voices, no arguing, no other breath but CaLarca's. It felt strange, and comforting.

CaLarca flicked the switches to power the engine. A glimmer of shame went through her chest, but she removed it, like a surgeon, and focused on the numbers, the levels, the sky opening up in front of her.

Since her first day on board the *Arazura*, so many weeks ago, CaLarca had written a letter every day to Ganasan and Bennet. Sometimes it was just a few words; sometimes she told them what she'd learned, what she'd seen that day, and how sorry she was to have left them. Then, when she was finished writing the entry in her Lissome, she would read it over, absorb the words, and then delete the entire thing. She loathed the thought of anyone gaining insight into her vulnerability. But she needed the routine; she needed to maintain some contact to her former life, however much of a dream it was. She needed to believe that as she came up with the words, Ganasan and Bennet would hear them, somehow.

Inside the cockpit, CaLarca set a course for the west border checkpoint, several hundred kilometers away. It would take hours to cross the continent. But the coordinates were specific, as was the code included with them: *GBASC*.

Two days ago, the crew of the *Arazura* had been recovering from recent violent events; CaLarca was piloting the ship alone. The five letters flashed on the console. At the sight of it, CaLarca's blood shot through with fire, and she had to bar the door to the cockpit so no one would discover her hyperventilating.

GBASC: a code that she and Ganasan had set up long ago, an acronym to use, in case they were separated, to indicate they were living, in danger, or if it was safe to reunite.

Ganasan - Bennet - Alive - Safe - Come.

Her legs ached; she ran her hand over her thigh muscle, feeling the wires in the leggings, how they supported her limbs. Renzo had created a custom-built Stance-Control-Knee-Ankle-Foot-Orthosis for her weeks ago, when her wounds were healing and she couldn't walk. Guilt panged in her chest. When she explained it to Renzo, when she returned the *Arazura*, he would understand, more than any of them. They had always shared a guarded, but respectful friendship.

CaLarca stood up, stretching out her back, adjusting the accompanying SCKAFO brace around her lower back. She ran one hand over her braids, over and over again; the texture and the weight of them were comforting, somehow, as she stared out into the clouds. Her stomach burned. She turned her hand upwards, and focused. Her palm grew hot, then searing. She bit her lip and kept going, until she smelled metal, felt smoothness in her fingers, felt the heat start to dissipate.

She opened her eyes and looked down. A knife: four-inch blade, pearl-handled, twisting silver and gold design on the hilt. The same knife she'd made since she was a girl. She could create it with hardly a thought, now, after so many times. Why a knife? she wondered, and not for the first time. She didn't dream of knives, but that image was buried deep within her, it seemed. A reflection of her propensity for violence, perhaps. Or maybe some kind of glimpse into the future. Either way, the manifestation did its trick; the Nadi energy that was smoldering at her core was gone.

Now she could focus. Checking the dashboard, CaLarca noted that the *Arazura* had four hours of fuel left. Where would replacement cells be stored? And what else was onboard that she could use?

The door slid open, yet CaLarca hesitated on the threshold of Phaira's cabin. There were strange vibrations in that space, warnings, a shadow of a voice, pricking at her skin. In their two months on the *Arazura*, CaLarca and Phaira managed to co-exist, even work together a few times for the greater good. Phaira had even travelled south, walked the scorched vineyards with her own two feet, searching for signs of Ganasan and Bennet. They fought as a team against the Red menace on the skerries.

Don't be stupid, she told herself. *Phaira would kill you if she had the opportunity.* When they first met, the blue-haired woman had voted to cast the severely injured CaLarca off the ship, but luckily, the others on the *Arazura* disagreed. Phaira had thrown insults like arrows at CaLarca, again and again, questioning her integrity, and she refused to even consider CaLarca's opinion on so many matters.

They weren't friends. They weren't even colleagues.

She wasted no time in riffling through the drawers and piles of clothing, swiping her hands under the mattress, checking the wall panels for secret latches. No sign of those ash-gray cigarettes, to her surprise. Phaira didn't have a stash of mekaline somewhere? CaLarca did find a handgun hidden under her mattress; firearms were still illegal in Osha, and she didn't need patrol tracking her down or the attention of the black market, but she still tucked it into the waistband of our SCKAFO.

There would be nothing in Cohen's room worth anything, she was certain.

Renzo... she would go into his space only if necessary.

That left Sydel's quarters, and the medical clinic within, filled with supplies that she could sell.

As CaLarca rummaged through the clinic drawers, a burning shame settled over her shoulders like a shawl. Sydel didn't deserve this; she didn't deserve anything that had happened over the past weeks. All because of who she came from, and what she potentially could mean to the future.

I will return these supplies, she promised to the silent clinic, taking the portable ultrasound and vials of medicine, and tucking them into a satchel.

Back in the cockpit, CaLarca checked the console; the autopilot was still engaged, still headed west, to the nearest Vendor

Mill. Three hours. Settling into the pilot seat, she popped open a compartment to her left: inside was a sleek syringe. One charge left. She had never used a REM injector before, and she hesitated at that syringe point at the crook of her elbow, but it was easy to click the trigger, and so quickly, she was waking again, one hour later, groggy and unbalanced, but the overwhelming fatigue far less. She hoped she would never have to use one again.

For the remaining two hours, CaLarca remained in the lower level of the *Arazura*. She had memorized a number of training modules, offensive and defensive measures, and she went through the motions, imaging various heads at the other end of her conjured knife. Kuri. The Red.

And whoever was waiting at those coordinates.

Yes, she was likely walking into a trap. Maybe Ganasan had been tortured into revealing their code. He and Bennet could still be dead, as reported. The memory of that moment, when she first heard of their bodies found in the alley, made it feel like her chest was cleaved open. So many nights, she'd lain awake, imagining the terror that her son must have felt; how he might have cried out for her, asked why she wasn't there to protect him. It didn't matter how much CaLarca argued with the ghost of her son, how many times she tried to explain that her return to Kings Canyon, her battered legs, the alliance with the crew of the *Arazura*, it was all to protect their family.

Sudden beeping, coming from upstairs. She ran to the cockpit. The console was flashing a series of letters and numbers. Connection code. Someone was trying to connect to the *Arazura*. Her heart squeezed until she thought she might collapse. She still had at least two hours to fly. She had to cover, she had to stay calm.

Her fingers shook as she made the connection. "Hello?"

"Is that CaLarca?"

Anandi Ajyo. The hacker girl. What if she figured out that CaLarca had stolen the *Arazura*? Anandi could shut down the engines from afar, she felt certain of it, or put out a bulletin for her arrest.

"Can you hear me? Are you still piloting?"

"I am," said CaLarca, steadying her voice. "I volunteered, so the others could rest."

"Renzo's not picking up his Lissome, I got worried that - "

"Because he is exhausted," CaLarca interrupted. "They asked me to keep to the sky. Things are still so unsettled."

"You seem reasonable, CaLarca, can't you convince them to stop getting involved in stupid situations?"

"You forget that I was equally involved in the Red situation," CaLarca couldn't help her retort. "I need to focus on flying. I'm still new to all this, and I want to ensure - " she stumbled a little on the words. "I want to keep the *Arazura* in perfect condition."

"That's probably the nicest thing I've heard you say." Anandi sighed. "Fine. Just let Renzo know I have to talk to him."

"I will. Take care." Then CaLarca cursed herself for being so polite. That was completely against her nature; it would only draw suspicion from the girl as to why CaLarca would even say such a thing. But it was too late to do anything about it now.

She ran her hand over the *Arazura's* controls, its smooth, cool surface. Her memories clicked back to the lessons in the cockpit with Renzo, and his confidence in her ability, even as she faltered.

"You have to feel the ship," he told her. "It's not just about buttons and levers. When I'm flying her, I'm part of her. She moves when I move, she reacts when I react. It's the way she's made. She's my girl, but you can be just as close."

It was a weirdly intimate moment: his view of CaLarca as a friend worthy of taking possession of something he cared for, maybe the thing he cared about the most in the world.

I meant what I said, CaLarca thought, staring over the horizon. *Perfect condition, as perfect as I can keep it. I promise.*

Within the hour, the *Arazura* crossed over Midland, where Sydel was from. Soon, she would hit the west border. Nerves bubbled up in her stomach. Like most people in Osha, CaLarca knew little about the territory. Infrastructure crumbled in the heat. Nothing would grow in the soil, and there were scores of dangerous, poisonous animals in the West, so said rumors. The only part she had ever seen was Kings Canyon, twenty-five years ago, and then only weeks ago, but that was near the Midland border, not out in the savage wastelands. Most maps left the left side of the continent blank, save for some ridges for mountains, there were so few people actually living in the area, and no established cities or towns. Historically, the only entry on the West was the civil war: two desert factions laying claim to a patch of land, causing some rumblings. The military got involved, that much she remembered. But the struggle only lasted a few weeks, and then nothing. There were so many other events happening in Osha: murders, political races, waves of crime in the East, all of which drew more focus. She wondered, now, about those factions: who they were, what they were fighting over, and if she would encounter them upon landing. She didn't know if there were other Vendor Mills in the West, or places to buy fuel cells, or even if there were any M-purification tablets to create safe water to drink. She was flying into a black hole, where anyone could be on the other side. They could be separatists. They could shoot her down from the sky for invading their space.

Stop being dramatic, CaLarca lectured herself. What could be worse than what she had already gone through? She had already faced down Kuri Nimat, and gotten sweet, though brief revenge, when she stabbed him through the ribs. She had taken part in the takedown of the Red, formerly Shantou Lyung, that genetically modified monster. Her legs were fully healed. Her Nadi and Eko skills had grown stronger. And the *Arazura* was outfitted with several security measures; even if there was some kind of attack, she could cloak the ship, and fly away, even lock herself inside.

She repeated all of those facts to herself, again and again, as the ship flew on.

II.

Docking magnets clicked into place. CaLarca took a few moments to gather her courage, to pull her grey hood over her head (Phaira's hood, she dimly remembered, clothes borrowed so long ago) before heading to the exit.

Outside, the Vendor Mill was small, in disrepair, and desolate. There were only a few merchants in magenta robes, half-heartedly showing their wares. The air was hot and full of sand, so dry that CaLarca's throat grew parched in seconds. She pulled her scarf over her nose, and her hood lower, gesturing for the attendant. "Replace the cells," she ordered. "Make sure they aren't draining too fast."

Would the ship be recognized? Would the siblings already have a bulletin out for her bounty? CaLarca worked to remain calm as she waited for the new fuel cells to be installed, resisting the urge to dart her gaze in all directions, for any sign of cameras, flashing knives, secret threats. She had no choice; this could be the last Vendor Mill for miles. She should get some water, some meal packs, maybe some ammunition for that handgun, if anyone was selling in secret...

"Can I get a ride?" A man swung into her view, his clothes dirty and ripped. "I'm safe," he added. "I just need to- "

"No," CaLarca said.

"I'll pay you. Please, I'm just going - "

"I don't want the rana, nor the company," she shot back.

The man's eyes flashed. "Come on, why can't you just - "

The knife was in her hand before he had a chance to finish. She saw the pulse in his throat before he backed away, yelping and sputtering.

CaLarca caught sight of the attendant watching from the rear of the *Arazura*, eyebrow raised. She glared at him until he looked away.

Woman travelling alone, in a shiny new ship, heading into isolated territory, she lectured herself. She shouldn't have stopped and made her presence known. What if pirates followed, ready to shoot her down?

Finally, finally, the cells were replaced, the attendant was paid, and the *Arazura's* engines were firing again. She was lifting into the air, she was safe and on her way through the West. No one followed, no matter how many times she checked the skies, and the land below. Nothing, nowhere. She tried to breathe, but she couldn't stop searching.

Soon, CaLarca saw the outlines of Kings Canyon. How far away it all seemed, how insignificant her three months underground, twenty-five years ago, where all this NINE drama started. Now she was flying past it, in a stolen airship, on her way to recover her dead husband and son.

The coordinates drew closer. Desert turned into rock, a few settlements here and there, widely spread out. The lack of population made CaLarca feel uneasy. The air was growing thicker with sand, she realized, the *Arazura* rocking in the rising wind. There was a light, far in the distance, that beckoned to her. She switched off the autopilot, and braced her hands on the throttle, easing it down as she released the landing gear. It would be good to be on the ground again. Peering into the horizon, she saw nothing but sand, and that single light, drawing closer, and highlighting the outline of a small, isolated building. Her heart thumped.

Finally on the ground, the *Arazura* hissed into silence, the engines pinging as they cooled. CaLarca packed her few items into one of Phaira's satchels, plus the handgun, and the supplies from the clinic. If needed, she could abandon the *Arazura* and travel on foot. She could sell the medical equipment and medicine if she needed any rana; if there were remote settlements, they were probably lacking in basic supplies, and could use what she had to offer. Whatever was out there, she could manage.

CaLarca pulled her hood over her head, checked her leg braces, and made her way to the exit. She didn't look into any of the cabins as she passed them. She didn't look back at any part of the *Arazura*, not until her feet hit the ground. Then she couldn't help but glance at it, looking for any signs of scratches or damage. It was still perfect. Just like Renzo would have wanted.

Through the rising winds of sand (how had it risen so fast?) a shadow was approaching.

Squinting, CaLarca ground her feet down, and let the heat pool into her free hand, the other gripping the satchel over her shoulder.

A man, she soon realized, a man with a flapping tunic and trousers, head and face wrapped with a scarf.

"Sandstorm," the man was yelling at her, gesturing at her to follow. "Take shelter."

"Who are you?" she hollered back. Her mouth was full of sand, and she coughed, covering her own nose with the collar of her shirt.

"No time!" she heard his reply, over the roar of the wind.

"No! I'll go back to my ship!" Though now, with the rising storm, she could hardly see in front of her.

Suddenly, a hard hand grabbed her wrist. She gasped, inhaling more sand, and doubled over coughing.

The hand pulled. She bent her head into the wind, and let herself be dragged forward, past the light, into a swallowing darkness.

The sudden drop of wind and pressure. The metal clang of a door.

Her core was burning. Danger. She was a woman, alone in a strange place. Nadi was only too eager to pool into her hand. That pearl-handled knife manifested behind her back.

A flicker of light. She was in an empty room.

"Cyrah."

CaLarca lunged.

Then she was stumbling backwards, her feet tripping over each other. Her back hit the wall.

Then her arm lifted, as if pulled by a rope, and she couldn't control it, nor the speed of which the knife turned and plunged into her chest.

She couldn't breathe. She couldn't see.

Finally, the black spots in her vision cleared.

The hilt of the knife was wedged under her armpit, the blade lodged in the wall, cold metal against the inside of her bicep.

Her body shook as she lifted her arms (she could move them again!) and slid down to her knees.

Across the room, the man unwrapped the scarf from his face. It was a man in his sixties, with brown, lined skin, and grey-streaked hair pulled back from his face. "I don't want to do that again," he told her. "But I will if you can't control yourself."

"Who-who are you?" she demanded, trying not to pant.

The man gave a faint smile. "You don't recognize me. I suppose you wouldn't. I lost the beard some time ago."

Beard?

Voss. VOSS. Zarek Voss.

Her mind raced with panic. *The one who looked like a professor. The one who rallied us to break free. The one who stabbed Joran to death, who made me run across the desert until I passed out.*

It all made sense. First Kuri, then Shantou; Voss was the last one left of the original NINE, so of course he was the final villain to overcome. The one behind it all; sending Kuri and Shantou after Sydel; burning her farm to the ground; tricking her into thinking her family was alive - her family - her family, it was all a lie...

"No, Cyrah."

She stiffened at the sound of his voice, and glanced up.

Voss was watching her with a weary sadness. "That's not it at all."

She could barely get the words out. "Which - what parts?"

"All of it."

His hand swung. Something glimmered, heading in her direction.

She caught it; a Lissome, a scratched, older model.

Above her fist, a video screen unzipped, startling her.

A recording started: black visual projection; she couldn't see anything.

Then she gasped as Ganasan came into the frame.

He was heavily bearded, and pacing a stone floor back and forth, holding a large bundle against his shoulder, patting it with one hand.

Then Ganasan's other hand flipped to face the camera. Something was written on his palm.

Letters. G-B-A-S-C.

Their code, she realized, before the screen was sucked back into the Lissome.

"They're alive," she choked.

"Yes," Voss confirmed. "They're with Joran."

She must have misheard him. "They're - what?"

"Joran has them," he repeated.

"Joran Asanto is dead," she sputtered. "You stabbed him in Kings."

"It's a ruse," Voss said. "All of it."

"You're lying!"

But even as she shouted the words, CaLarca knew he wasn't lying. Not unless he was able to control the energy that radiated off him; he shimmered with pale yellow, and there wasn't a trace of grey, that telltale sign of deception that CaLarca could see.

But how could it be true? How was that possible?

Voss's voice broke through her racing thoughts. "Let me help you up. Take a drink. I know it's a lot to process."

She let herself be hauled to her feet and guided to a stone bench. A copper mug was in her hand. Water, clean and cold, shocked her throat.

"You sent me the coordinates," she finally said.

"I did."

"Why to this place?"

"Because no one knows about it," Voss said. "It's a border checkpoint established during the civil war, long since abandoned. I only discovered it by accident, years ago. Thought it would be a good place to disappear someday."

"But Ganasan gave you our code," CaLarca said. "Why would he do that? Did you... force him?"

"No, it was his idea. I think he knew that you wouldn't come without it. Or believe me without video proof." He smiled then, a crooked, sad smile. "It's funny how you two are together after all this time. Can't say that I predicted that."

The wind howled outside. CaLarca tried to equate the man in front of her with the terrifying man from Kings Canyon. Her memories flashed in sequence: their introduction, his fascination with her Nadi abilities, his outburst to Joran, accusing him of ulterior motives, then Voss's persuasion to make CaLarca confess where the hidden door to the outside was, how his body was hunched over Joran's, in the sandy canyon, the hand on her head as she retched, his voice telling her to run.

She should run now. Even with the sandstorm, she should find her way back to the *Arazura*. But what then?

A shadow passed over her.

The top of Voss's head was in front of her, as he knelt on one knee, as if she were a queen.

"Go ahead," he prodded. "Search my memory. Whatever, and wherever you choose to look. Learn the truth."

CaLarca stared at the crown of his head. She could generate a knife and stab him through the throat; she could still feel the haze of Nadi in her hand. How easy it would be to make another. She could bash him over the neck; she had gained much strength over the last few months. She could torture out the truth. What if she dove into his memories via Eko and he trapped her there?

Slowly, she peered into the edges of his mind, piercing the veil, and seeing the first glimmers of memory, how they danced along the curves of his brain, waving as though in water. There were no burnt areas, no charred memories. It was all there, begging to be accessed.

She would remain on the outskirts, she determined, squinting in the faint light.

The truth. Finally, maybe, the truth.

III.

*Z*arek Voss laid his head against Joran Asanto's shoulder, studying all the diagrams. Sheets of paper flooded the two desks, with such small writing that Voss had to squint to read.

"Construction is underway," Joran told him. "I'll need your help to remove the contractors' memories at the end of the project, of course," he added, tapping Voss on the forehead.

"Estimated start date?"

"Two weeks, ideally. I just need one more Eko," Joran said. "Then we have a perfect group of participants. Nine test subjects, to experiment with NINE. Poetic, really."

Voss lifted his head, suddenly in doubt. "Wait - have you included Tehmi in this?"

"We need one of each skillset," Joran explained. "And I need a second Insynn to compare notes. I've only found the boy, Ganasan Reed, so far. I thought it would be easier to find another Insynn."

Voss scowled, jealousy coursing through him. "Being underground is probably bad for the baby. What if something happens?"

Joran shrugged, pointing at a profile. "This one, Yann Qin, he's a physician, and he's agreed to help as needed with medical emergencies, for an added bonus, of course. Happy coincidence, isn't it? I'll make sure he has everything he needs. And if she has the baby underground, look at it this way: it's a tenth test subject to work with!" He sounded almost giddy.

This was the part of Joran Asanto that Voss sometimes found hard to love, that focus and drive that bulldozed over everything else. Maybe it was because Joran came from money and was used to the world adjusting to accommodate. Then again, it was because of the money that they could even do this experiment, what they'd longed to do since they first met, twenty years ago. Voss was the newest intern in the paranormal research department at a tiny university. Joran Asanto was the head researcher, the lead funder, young and handsome. Voss felt the jolt of attraction as he walked through the door.

Confessions quickly followed: they each had strange, unexplainable gifts, which fueled their desire to learn about the supernatural. Voss could hear thoughts, and see energy waves, while Joran had some power of persuasion; he could get anyone to do what he wanted, whether it was a smile returned, permission for his experiments, a table at a restaurant. Even better, his income was unlimited, from what Voss could see, and Voss was thrilled to be taken care of, to be able to do whatever he wanted, scientifically, or personally, in Osha.

Even when Joran picked up Tehmi Shovann from a corner and installed her as his public partner (to appease his family, Joran reasoned, so they would leave them alone to work), it was still Voss that Joran came to in his need. They were on the brink of something amazing, and they would discover it together, make their names known throughout Osha. Take power by name or money or both. Their nights were filled with theories on NINE abilities from decades before, myths that could be truths, experimental theories on psychic abilities and kinetic visions, into studies of the brain and energy paths in the body, how it was all connected, and how it had been clear to them both for some time that they were not the only ones in Osha with abilities.

There were others, hidden somewhere. Joran was passionate about finding them, and soon so was Voss. They grew hungry with the potential for evolution. During their relationship, Joran and Voss performed experiments on each other. The more they worked, the more isolated they became, only speaking with each other. Over the years, Voss gained the ability to manipulate the energy he saw, and Joran grew more persuasive with less effort; he could get what he wanted with just a look now. They learned that, when injected into those with NINE abilities, a specific chemical compound caused severe blistering on the lower back that later scarred in a swirl pattern.

They needed more test subjects. Joran and Voss approached people in the community, trying to see if they could prompt a NINE reaction. Complaints were made. The university had grumbled for years about the lack of published work, professional respect and behavior, and now the noises grew louder. Eventually, they refused Joran's rana and shut down the paranormal research program for good, citing the need for more relevant studies. It didn't matter to Voss and Joran; it was better to continue without the old ghouls and their restraints.

Soon after, Joran had an idea: a closed study, intensive retreat over three months, using a variety of different methods to test the boundaries of these abilities. Controlled environment, various test subjects, substantial payout. They just needed to find the candidates.

He'd gotten the idea, strangely enough, from Tehmi's pregnancy. The woman had been around for years with rare interaction, other than public appearances as Joran's wife, but there was growing pressure for him to provide an heir to his fortune, so they went the artificial route. Voss shouldn't have been jealous, but he was, even though he was in the same room as Joran and Tehmi, watching the insemination process, trying not to grind his teeth.

In the moment she was announced to be pregnant, Tehmi was much more present than she ever was. She would now be a mother, and forever connected to Joran in a way Voss wasn't. Now they were forming a unit, and Voss would never be a part of it.

Thank goodness the procedure took the first time.

And Joran was more energized than ever, not with the anticipation of his offspring, but how they should be studying the influence of puberty and environment.

Not only that, Joran told Voss, but the effect of pregnancy on NINE. Because Tehmi, to Voss's great surprise, turned out to be an Insynn, with a gift for precognition. Only a recent development, triggered by the pregnancy, it seemed, but perfect timing.

Tehmi agreed to participate. Her eyes were unfocused when she said yes, Voss noticed, and, for the first time, he wondered what she was thinking.

Finding other participants, however, took far longer than either Voss or Joran anticipated. They scanned police reports, gossip in towns across Osha, searching for any signs of NINE activity. They found potentials again and again, but every time they confronted someone, pleaded with them, tried to show them they were the same, they fled. Everyone was terrified to confirm any NINE within them, whether child or adult.

Eventually, it took Joran's persuasion and threats of exposure to get anywhere. And payment, of course. When they told the people that there was rana, faces changed, and deals were struck: come to Kings Canyon for three months, live there, and leave rich. When Voss stopped begging, and Joran flashed rana, they all said yes.

And now they were here, with plans drawn, construction underway, two weeks away from the start date, and Voss couldn't shake the queasiness in his stomach. He reached into one of the petri dishes, taking the shard of metal between thumb and forefinger. It looked like nothing, like a silver grain of rice. "I still don't know about this," he muttered.

"It'll be fine," Joran soothed. "They won't know it's in there. We'll put them under, and then inject it. I've been training Tehmi on it."

"I still don't understand its purpose, though."

"It's simple," Joran said. "The implant is a tracker, and it's got enough of an electrical pulse to disrupt the brain and shut down the nervous system, in case there's any trouble."

"But it's also a potential kill-switch," Voss pointed out. "Its position, so close to the brain stem, will be instant death, if the right reaction is triggered."

"Yes, that's true."

"I just don't know -"

"This is such an unknown operation, Voss. Who knows what will happen after these three months?" Joran countered, his voice hushed and serious. "We need to know where these people go afterwards, what they are compelled to do after the time is up. If we give them growth, and they become too dangerous, there needs to be a failsafe to protect the public."

"And if someone with Nadi knows it's in there, and makes it move on its own?" Voss shot back. "You don't need to flick the switch to kill someone, if you can make it tear through their brain."

Joran quirked an eyebrow. "Is that what you're threatening to do?"

"No, but it's a valid question."

"It's an interesting one, to be sure. And you're right. I suppose you could, if you were strong enough, and had enough ability to physically move things, not just the energy around them."

Which isn't me, Voss thought, a sting in his chest. He felt insulted, though he didn't quite know why.

Instead, Voss turned away from the table, and fingered the beads around his wrist in thought, the bracelet that Voss had given to him only a month ago, for their twenty-year anniversary. Beads forged in the West with strange sand that, when heated and cooled into glass, provided a black reflection, eerie and utterly fascinating.

He jumped at the sudden squeeze of his hand.

"I need you to be okay with this," Joran whispered. "I can't do this without your support. Just think of what we'll witness, what we'll create when this is finished. This is a bigger leap forward in evolution than any in recent history."

A rush of warmth filled Vosst. "Who's the last Eko?"

"I'm looking at a girl from the south-east. Fourteen years old. Funny enough, I know her parents, the CaLarcas. I went to university with the wife ages ago. They've been secretly trying to find some treatment options for their daughter's 'disability.' I'm going to reintroduce myself and offer a solution."

"Just like that?" Voss couldn't help but ask.

Joran smiled. "I can be persuasive."

* * *

The easiest appearance to take on was that of the amiable elder, and Voss had the look secured, having grown out his beard, and letting a comfortable belly grow over his belt. Friendly. Non-threatening. And attached to no one, not even Joran. To maintain objectivity, Voss and Joran were acquaintances, nothing more, until things were more certain about the NINE recruits.

Voss watched from a corner as the selected seven wandered throughout the underground base, asking questions and scratching their skin, as if already feeling suffocated. Voss felt the same urge to escape to the outside. *It will pass*, he told himself. *Patience. Take stock of the participants, before they notice you watching. Follow the plan. It will be worth it.*

It was fascinating to watch the participants settle into a living routine, and eventually, reveal their hidden abilities. Most only had the sputterings of Eko, or generating Nadi energy. The children, especially, made Voss nervous. There were four in total; Ganasan, CaLarca and the twins, Shantou and Marette. All under the age of sixteen, all with those burn swirls on the small of their back, soon to be a deep orange-brown scar. Why had their parents allowed them to come to this place? He wouldn't have. And, watching Tehmi from a distance, one hand on her smug belly, he wouldn't have let Tehmi in this place either, not if it were his baby she was carrying.

The green-haired girl, Cyrah CaLarca, fascinated him. The girl could actually manifest objects with her Nadi, something that Voss had never seen before. He put on his most kindly voice and asked as many questions as she was willing to answer, hard-nosed and suspicious as the girl was, and watched her during experiments. She reacted strongly to psychotropic drugs, the Nadi flaring in her so hot and so violent than her heart beat too fast, and the girl passed out. Voss raced to her side to draw out the access Nadi: middle knuckle pressed into her belly, energy sucking up through his veins, and setting his bones on fire. He refused to scream with pain. Afterwards, everyone treated him with reverence, especially Kuri and Shantou. But when he managed to get Joran alone, and told him about the lingering pain, Joran soothed Voss's worried words, and gave him a reassuring kiss. That intimate touch, after so long, diverted Voss's thoughts for a while.

But soon, too soon, worries crept back in. The group was advancing rapidly, growing more and more powerful. Things were changing for Voss, too. His brain felt rubbery, like cells eased apart and snapping into new places, the more he looked into the black eyes of CaLarca, or the scared brown eyes of Ganasan, the ten-year old that Joran had managed to recruit into the experiment.

And groups were forming, like Kuri Nimat, the young man with the shock of black hair, his chin held too high to be humble, and one of the twins, Shantou Lyung, with the red hair. Between them, there was a strange, almost perverse attraction in the air (how old was she again?). Taking them aside one night, Voss reminded them that there were to be no relations during this period. To his surprise, they both started crying, and begged him to keep their relationship a secret. After that night, Kuri and Shantou were always close to him, thanking him under breath for his protection.

A month into the program, Voss was shaken awake.

Above him, Joran's face was half in shadow from the candle he held in one hand. "Come on," he instructed. "It's time for the next phase."

What phase was that? Voss couldn't remember, but he roused himself from the warm bed, and followed Joran up the stairwell.

Kuri and Shantou looked up when they entered; huddled together, half-asleep and terrified. Joran settled onto the floor next to the couple. Voss hesitated. Was this some kind of intervention? He hadn't told Joran about Kuri and Shantou, but perhaps it was obvious.

"Sit, Voss. Please." Joran gestured at the remaining spot in the circle. "I have something to share with you three."

Three?

"You've learned about Eko, and Nadi," Joran began. "And you've learned about Insynn, or precognition. Now, the three of you are ready to learn about the fourth ability."

"The fourth," Shantou repeated in a whisper.

"Yes," Joran said. "It's been referred to as 'Nyx.'"

"Doesn't 'nix' mean to obliterate?" Kuri asked, as Shantou gripped his hand. Voss wished he could do the same with Joran.

"In a sense, yes," Joran said. "But it's more subtle and beautiful than that."

He glanced behind him, and Voss was surprised to see Tehmi's pregnant silhouette in the shadows.

She took two steps towards them.

Then she stopped, quarter-turning on the ball of her foot, and started to walk in a dragging side-step. No one spoke; the only sound was Tehmi's bare feet, sliding across the floor.

Then she turned again, her back to the group, walking backwards.

Finally, when she was about to step into the center of the circle, she stopped moving.

From his seat, Voss stared up at Tehmi's profile; her nostrils were flared, her face flushed. Still, she said nothing.

"You made her do that," Shantou said. "Did you make her do that?"

"I did," Joran confirmed.

"How?"

"Very similar to Eko," Joran said. "Much like finding the threads of memories, it's finding the threads of the body, and coaxing them to move independently of its host."

"Is that all you can do with it? Make people move?" Shantou asked, sounding less impressed. Voss felt a flash of anger at her arrogance. Didn't she realize what she was being shown?

"No," Joran told the girl. "With practice, you can control the speech of a person, or speak through them. When you discover the right parts of the brain to connect to."

"How do you know what parts of the brain are safe to touch?" Kuri asked, a strange glint in his eye.

"By exploration," Joran smiled. "And experimentation on each other - "

The question burst out of Voss: "Maybe we shouldn't be doing this."

Everyone turned to face him, surprised.

Voss stared at Joran, wishing that they were both Ekos, that they could communicate without voices. These two children, they weren't ones to be trusted with this kind of knowledge, he could sense it. Couldn't Joran?

"You can, and you will," Joran said quietly. "It's vital that you master this skill. Because I'm trusting the three of you to watch over the others, from here on out, and ensure that they are safe, and controlled."

Voss didn't know what to say. It was a strange task to lay on these two young, unstable people, without telling Voss about it first. What did Joran expect them to do?

"What do you mean by controlled?" Kuri asked.

"There are powerful people in this study," Joran said. "And as we continue, if it appears that someone has grown dangerous, then we have to protect the integrity of the group."

Tehmi reappeared then, holding a cage with a rat inside. Joran reached into the cage and withdrew the critter. The rat climbed up his arm, its wormy tail wrapped around his wrist.

Joran's eyes narrowed.

The rat froze, its squeak cut-off, one tiny claw lifted.

Then the rat tipped backwards, and hit the floor with a sickening thump.

Kuri, Shantou and Voss stared at the tiny corpse. Joran pushed its body aside, so Tehmi could pick it back up again and waddle back into the darkness.

"You did that," Shantou breathed. "You killed it."

Voss was speechless. He'd never seen Joran do that before, not in twenty years. What else was he hiding from Voss?

"Practice," Joran said. "It only takes practice to know where to push."

* * *

But it was a mistake. Voss recognized every sign of danger, from the greediness in which Kuri and Shantou lapped up the information that Joran provided, with how callously they killed rat after rat with a gleeful expression at night, when everyone was asleep.

It was bleeding into the day sessions with the rest of the group, too. Kuri kept pushing the others, trying to peer into their memories. Surprisingly, it was the youngest of the group, Ganasan, who put up the most vocal fight.

"I said no!" the boy had shouted. "And I won't say it again!"

Along with everyone else on the floor, Voss turned at the noise.

Kuri raised his hands in defense. "We're just talking."

"You're supposed to focus on the Nadi experiments," Joran reminded him, a warning in his voice.

Kuri's eyes narrowed. "I'm trying to help him."

Then he addressed the boy. "Gani, just go and ask Shantou. She did it, and it didn't hurt."

"Don't call me Gani," the boy hollered." I don't care. You're not doing it, no matter what you threaten."

"You realize that I could just do it if I wanted to, and you couldn't stop me," Kuri said snidely.

"Stop it!" It was Tehmi, one hand on her belly, the other outstretched like some avenging angel. "He said no. Leave him alone. I mean it. He has a choice whether to -"

"Does he?" Voss burst out. "Does he really?"

Where did those words come from?

Tehmi glared at him. "Of course," she said, a warning in her voice. "He's just a child."

"Unfortunate for them to be involved in this," Voss couldn't stop the words from spilling out. "But they are, and we are, and we both know that there's no freedom, Tehmi."

No one spoke. Voss stole a look at Joran. Joran's expression was one of heartbreak, like his trust had been shattered.

Then Joran stepped to the center of the room. "You all agreed to a contract," he said. "To payment, for three months of service, under the rules given to you on entry. Behave yourself, and step away from each other. Now!"

Then Tehmi gasped, her hands cradling her swollen stomach as her knees buckled. Joran ran to her, taking advantage of the distraction, even though Voss could see that Tehmi was faking the pain, how her contorted face went back to its neutral expression as she whispered in Joran's ear.

They were united.

But Joran surprised him again that night, taking him aside with a wide smile. "A great development," he told Voss in the shadows. "It's only natural that Kuri would rebel in this group, with his growing power. And even better, they trust you."

"I don't understand what your goal is. What our goal is," Voss added, with some indignation. His thoughts raced: *When did I become one of your test subjects to manipulate?*

"Therein lies the beauty," Joran said. "We are caught in the current, and the cold ride is unlike anything else. Let it go, Voss. Let what happens, happen."

* * *

"We need to leave," Kuri said.

Voss kept his expression neutral. Only an hour after his secret discussion with Joran, Shantou and Kuri had appeared like pale specters, and wordlessly gestured for Voss to follow them. They locked themselves in Kuri's room on the third floor, and in a whisper, shared their concerns with Voss.

Joran had ulterior motives, they were sure of it. They didn't need to be there any longer, not after all they had learned. They were stronger than him, stronger than anyone there, and the longer they stayed, the more they were certain that something bad would happen. Voss didn't ask if they were afraid of someone hurting them, or if they might hurt others, but both seemed likely.

Let what happens, happen. Joran's words floated through his brain.

"We need to get outside. We need to get away from here."
Kuri put his arm around Shantou, who had remained silent the
whole time. Her long red hair covered her face, and they were
both thinner, with a hungry look in their eye, since they had
learned about Nyx. Voss hated every second of the sensation
of using Nyx on that rat, how it made him shuddery and weak.
What was its toll on Kuri and Shantou?

"I can't help you," Voss said. "None of us have the capacity
to leave."

"Joran does." A thin, whispering voice came from under that
red hair. "He leaves all the time."

Voss frowned. "He doesn't. I assure you, he doesn't."

"How are you so certain?"

A cold jolt went through Voss. He didn't know. He didn't
know anything.

Voss stood up, surprising Kuri and Shantou, and left the
room. He broke into all three floors of the underground base,
but he couldn't find Joran anywhere, not on any floor. *It's impossible*, he told himself, as he searched each room, each corridor,
to no avail. Tehmi appeared once, asking what was wrong, but
she averted her eyes when he asked where Joran was.

Shantou was right. Joran was in contact with the outside
world, while the rest of them festered in the underground, under the pretense that no one, including Joran, would be able to
leave until the end of the ninety-day period. Joran had never
shown him the way outside. He was using Voss like he was the
others. He was a test subject, a commodity to be prodded. Joran
didn't really love Voss. He just loved the fact that Voss would
always come back to him.

He banged his fist on the wall of the second floor. At the loud echo, he heard the sound of a gasp. Light appeared in the darkness. Voss squinted; it was the teenage girl CaLarca, glaring at him, her mouth scrunched tight, and shoulders up around her ears. *Spying on me. Following me. Little brat.*

His thoughts turned. *She's so powerful. Why didn't Joran bring her into the group to learn Nyx?*

Because she's not weak-minded, came the quick response in his brain. *Because Joran only showed the ability to those that he would still be able to control in the end.*

It just made him angrier, and he hit the wall again. The impact reverberated up the wall. CaLarca disappeared. Voss rubbed his knuckles and slid to the floor.

I'm not weak. I'm not his to control. I'm not staying here any longer.

An idea struck him. Maybe the girl could help him. She was always watching everyone. Maybe she had seen Joran leave.

The next day, Voss cornered CaLarca, and before she could protest, he pushed her into his room. Inside, Shantou and Kuri sat next to each other on the bed, holding hands. Voss stood in front of the door, barring her exit. "I have a favor to ask of you, CaLarca. You're always wandering. You know every corner of this place, I'd wager."

The girl's voice was haughty, but scared. "I can't break out of here, if that's what you want."

Amazing! Voss couldn't help but laugh a little. "Perceptive little thing, aren't you. But powerful. One of the most powerful ones here. What do you think about this experiment, CaLarca?"

CaLarca shuffled her feet. "I don't know. It's fine."

"And what do you think about our hosts?" Voss pressed. How much did she know? How much had she guessed?

"They're okay."

"You can sense lies," Voss told her. "You told me once, in conference. That's related to Nadi, but you've developed some Eko talents, I believe."

"I - maybe."

"It's okay. We're the same as you," Voss reassured her. "We're changing too. Growing stronger. It's amazing, isn't it?"

The girl nodded.

"But for what purpose? Why are we here?"

"To learn from each other," CaLarca recited.

"And then what?"

"We go home."

"Do you really think that's the case?" Voss pressed. "At the end of this, we just leave? Go our own separate ways, with a bag full of rana and powerful abilities? Is that logical?"

"I - I don't know," she stammered.

"Where's Joran right now, CaLarca?"

"I don't know. Somewhere, of course."

"I would wager," Voss said, a nasty edge to his words. "If you searched all three floors, you wouldn't find a trace of him."

"That's not possible."

"Were you put to sleep when you first arrived, for medical testing?" Voss challenged.

CaLarca's fingers touched the back of her head. Shantou and Kuri echoed her movements.

"Something was implanted in you. In all of us," Voss said.

It wasn't true; he had no implant of course, but he needed to show solidarity with them.

"I - I can't - I don't want to talk about this," CaLarca stammered, backing away.

When Kuri went to go after her, Voss told him no, and let CaLarca pass, calling after her in a final, gleeful lash: "You will. Soon enough, you will."

* * *

After that night, everything happened so fast.

Tehmi went into labor. Voss sat with Joran outside the room, and they talked like they used to, before all this started.

"I'm sorry to keep secrets from you," Joran said, running a hand down Voss's arm. Infuriatingly, Voss felt a spark deep within from the touch. "But it's time to disappear."

Voss froze. Had Joran overheard the secret meetings? "What - what do you mean?"

"We have the controlled environment results of what can be achieved. Now I want to see what happens when pressure and mortal decisions are added into the mix."

"You're having a baby in there," Voss pointed out.

But Joran waved his hand, his eyes focused on a spot on the wall. "Everything is about to implode. The experiment is about to end, so I want to use it to its full advantage. Be ready. Start carrying a knife. When you need it, you'll find an exit out from CaLarca."

Voss shook his head again and again, sputtering with confusion.. "What are you - this is too much - these young people, you're manipulating them -"

"As are you," Joran said. "And have from the beginning, before you got this sudden streak of morality. This is all for the greater good. How can you forget that?"

At the words, Voss's mind grew slow and dreamy, and everything Joran said made sense, somehow. Was it Nyx, or something else that was altering his mind? Voss couldn't say.

And had Joran known what was about to happen to Tehmi? Did he know it would be that night when everything fell apart?

Because he was nowhere in sight that next morning, when a hysterical Shantou came to Voss, dragging him into Tehmi's room.

The sight of Tehmi's lifeless body in bed was jarring, but not altogether unpleasant. CaLarca was there, holding the squalling baby, and Kuri was wringing his hands over the bed, pleading with Voss to help. "We need to get out out," he repeated again and again. "We have to find a way."

CaLarca.

Voss turned to stare at the girl with the green braids, who shrank back.

"It's time to leave," Voss said loudly, feeling like an actor in a play. "Help us, CaLarca. Free us."

CaLarca shook her head, clutching the baby.

"She doesn't know anything," Shantou broke in. "We need to think about what to say to Joran."

Voss focused on CaLarca's brain: the spots that quivered, that he could alter.

I hate you, Joran, for making me do this.

"You don't want to stay," he recited. "You want to run away and forget that any of this ever happened. You want to forget about all of us. Start your life over on your terms, not theirs, or your parents. Yours. Let it go. You know you want to."

The pain and the nausea were rising, but he kept pushing the malleable brain threads, tying them together to form the thoughts he wanted, the confession that Joran wanted him to extract.

And finally, she was stammering, her words a tearful exhale: "The stairwell. Third floor platform. I think there's a secret door."

Zarek smiled. "Good girl."

CaLarca ran out of the room, her feet pounding down the corridor.

"I didn't mean to kill Tehmi, I swear," Kuri was whimpering, as Shantou patted his arm. "I just wanted the truth about what we're doing here. But she kept fighting me..."

"It's not your fault," Voss said. "It's Joran's. Come with me."

He headed for the stairwell, Kuri and Shantou squawking behind him.

On the third-floor platform, Voss ran his hands over the rock wall, and there it was: a door. All this time, and Voss had never noticed. He muttered curses as the door swung inwardly, and Voss walked into darkness. He felt the edge of the knife, the one Joran told him to carry on his person, against the outside of his thigh. He unsheathed it, one damp palm gripping the knife, the other outstretched to feel his way through the tunnel. He could hear Kuri and Shantou behind, their voices faint, but still following.

Voss broke into a run at the first crack in the dark, and burst into the sunlight, gasping at the dry wind, the brightness painful against his eyes.

Joran was standing in the middle of the canyon floor, fifty feet down rubble and rocks.

Voss couldn't stop his body from stumbling down the rocks to him, skidding and scraping his leg. Black spots swam in front of his eyes, as Joran's figure, then face drew clearer.

Joran's arms were behind his back, and he made no motion to move.

Voss's heart was exploding out of his chest.

His arm was lifting, the knife point reflected in the sun.

"Voss, no!" came Shantou's screech.

Joran's face was calm as Voss plunged the knife forward.

Voss heard something pop.

Red spilled over Joran's shirt, and Voss's arms.

Joran jerked his body to the ground. Voss was left standing.

Footsteps behind him, and the sound of horrified breath. Kuri and Shantou came into his peripheral view, streaked with red dust, staring at Joran's body on the canyon floor.

More sounds: voices from above.

Voss swiveled and craned his head to look. One hundred feet up, there were faces, terrified faces of adults and children, clustered together, watching the scene on the floor.

"They've seen us," Shantou whispered. "They'll call patrol."

"You hold them," Kuri hissed to her. "I'll wipe their minds."

Voss sensed Shantou and Kuri running away to the rocky escarpment, climbing up the rocks. But Voss couldn't see what was going on; there were too many tears in his eyes.

The sounds of screaming above grew loud, shatteringly loud.

A body fell on the rocks, landing with a crack and a splat.

There was a flash of green by the secret door, up the incline: CaLarca, on her hands and knees, heaving for breath.

Once again, his vision grew dark, and Voss couldn't stop himself from walking up the rubble, from putting a hand on her head: "Run, Cyrah."

He watched as CaLarca ran down the rocky incline and into the desert. He wondered when she might stop. He tried not to look at the woman's body strewn across the rocks, so few feet away, and tried to tune out the screams and pleas from above.

Then one by one, the voices went quiet.

Voss squinted in the sun, shielding his eyes to look up. Shantou and Kuri appeared over the edge of the canyon. Their hands were bloody, and their faces were masks of determination, and Voss could hear their thoughts: *We did it. We did it. We saved the group.*

Then the thoughts grew shaky, and high-pitched. *No. No. It's not possible.*

Voss turned to see Joran, rising to his feet.

Voss dropped the knife. He hadn't killed him, after all? But the blood, the pop, it was real, the pressure was real. Wasn't it?

Joran pulled his shirt open. A plastic packet of burst blood was strapped against his chest. The blade had sliced it open. That was the pop he heard. Not skin. Plastic.

It took a long time to reach the top of the canyon. Voss pushed forward, the heat of the sun bearing down, Joran's shadow behind him.

And the bodies came into view: sprawled across the sand, palms turned up and lifeless. Two adults, a man and a woman. Voss checked each of their pulses, trying not to recoil at how they were already growing cold.

And next to the bodies: four small children, three boys and one girl, claw marks on their skin, tears on their cheeks, breathing in little shudders. Alive. All with black hair, ranging in age from perhaps five to ten. Cousins, maybe, or siblings? Was this a family they had decimated?

Voss watched as Kuri drew his arm around Shantou and whispered something inaudible. But the red-haired girl just stared at Joran with a horrified expression.

"A test," Joran told her. "To see what you would do. You didn't stop Voss from killing me."

"I'm sorry, Joran," Kuri stammered out. "We didn't know - we would have -"

Joran waved his hand with irritation. Then he gestured at the bodies, his eyebrow raised.

"They won't remember what happened," Kuri assured him.

"They won't remember," Shantou repeated, as if in a dream.

Voss battled the urge to scream, or run away. But he couldn't leave, could he? He was a part of all of this scandal. Joran had them all by the throat. They had each other by the throat. The only choice was to stick together or make a vow to remain separate forever. And he sensed that Joran wasn't looking for that to happen.

"What do we do now?" Kuri asked.

There was a long pause.

"I need you two to get Tehmi," Joran finally said. "Bring her to the canyon floor."

Kuri and Shantou hesitated. Then they ran hand-in-hand, scrambling back down the rocky incline.

When they were out of range, Voss turned on Joran, barely able to contain his rage. "Why didn't you tell me? Why did you make me kill you?"

Then Joran's arms were around him. The fake blood seeped into Voss's shirt, as cold as Joran's lips, now kissing him on the forehead. "I'm sorry. But I've always planned to officially die and disappear after this experiment. I can do so much more if I leave the Asanto name behind. It's too well known, and too easy to blackmail. Of course, I've been storing rana in several secret accounts, under assumed names, for years now. ."

Voss could hardly comprehend what Joran was talking about. He couldn't stop looking at the corpses on the ground, and the little bodies that shook every few seconds. Joran saw nothing unusual about this? About any of this? What kind of man was he?

"I wonder if you have the same idea as me," Joran said, noting how Voss stared at the fallen family. "Wouldn't it be fascinating to study the long-term impact on these children? To see how they have changed after this experience? If they have been triggered in any way? Changed for the better, even? Perhaps the key to unlocking the potential in the average citizen is just to carve the path..."

Down on the canyon floor, Voss heard the sound of rustling. When he peered over the edge, he saw Kuri and Shantou struggling with a body-shaped bundle, wrapped in a white blanket.

"Are the others in there?" Joran called down.

"No. Ganasan, Yann and Marette are gone," Kuri hollered up to them. "They took the baby, I think." A sob caught in his throat, before he straightened, and laid the bundle carefully in the sand. Shantou looked over the body, like a red shadow.

"Gather some wood," Joran commanded. "When we burn the body, it will draw patrol to the location."

Kuri looked like he was going to vomit, even one hundred feet away. Shantou had no reaction, but started to sweep up twigs and branches, scattered across the canyon.

"Why would you - " Voss sputtered.

Joran gestured at his chest. "This packet was full of my own blood. When patrol are called to investigate, and find the body burned, the blood will be entered as evidence that I was also killed, and my body moved."

Then Joran bent down to the bodies of the two parents. For a moment, Voss thought that perhaps he was going to close their eyelids.

Then he saw Joran's hands rustling at the man's belt, and he withdrew a silver flask. Voss caught the faint stink of alcohol.

"Use this," Joran called down to Kuri, the flask glimmering in the sun as he tossed it. "It'll burn quicker.

V.

CaLarca withdrew from the memory. It was even worse than she remembered.

And Voss. She should strangle him where he sat.

Voss was staring at his hands. He had a bracelet on, she noticed, with dark round stones, the same from the vision. And familiar, somehow. The stones held some kind of meaning in her brain, but she couldn't place it. Had she seen it before?

"Even when he was free of his name, his wife, and his reputation, even with the successes he saw in Kings, Joran grew obsessed with those children who lived," Voss said, standing up. "He's stayed close to them all this time. Changed his name, his background, infiltrated their ranks. Even took their last name as his own."

"Who? Who is he now?"

Voss smiled thinly. "He's been known as 'Bianco Sava' for some time now."

Bianco Sava. She knew that name. Was that Theron Sava's handler? Wasn't he burned in some alleyway? That was really Joran?

"He wanted to understand the long-term effects of NINE manipulation on the brain," Voss muttered, his voice thick with shame. "I'm sorry to say that it took me a long time to work up the courage to leave him, and all of it behind. Twenty-five years. I have no excuse."

CaLarca couldn't think of what to say.

"He's been recruiting. Travelling the continent on Sava business for the past fifteen years," Voss continued. "But he was the one who put the idea in Keller Sava's head to hunt down the originals. I don't know what his endgame is; he never told me all the details, but I fear it's a showdown of some kind. It could be all-out war on Osha."

CaLarca was silent for a long time. Then she spoke: "The second N of the NINE acronym. Nyx. You can do it."

"I let it go, just a little bit, with you. You saw black spots in front of your eyes. You couldn't control the direction of your blade. If I wanted to, I could have killed you by your own hand. Made it look like an accident. Trust me when I say I hated every second of using it, and I still feel like I'm going to be sick."

Something clicked in CaLarca's head. "That was why that woman went over the cliff."

"Yes."

"That's how you made me run away, when you put your hand on my head. I wouldn't have moved, I didn't dare to move, but then I couldn't stop."

"Yes."

"And that's how I ended up at the bottom of that pit," CaLarca concluded. "There was no evidence that I'd been pushed. It was like I just walked over the edge, of my own free will."

"It's very possible. I was not a part of that. But it sounds like something Kuri and Shantou would do, out of desperation. Or by Joran's command."

"On Toomba," CaLarca said. "When we were in the mountains, and Kuri showed up in disguise, he was asking for ac-

cess to the Asanto inheritance, through Sydel's blood and recognition. Why would he do that, if Joran is still alive?"

"Because he's not alive," Voss said. "He gave up the Asanto
name twenty-five years ago. But before he officially died, his
family established a trust for any offspring. It's still valid. Now
he sent Kuri to try and access it, through Sydel."

"Does he even care that it's his daughter?"

Voss gave her a look that was a mixture of pity and disbelief.

"Why didn't you stop him?" CaLarca accused. "You just ran
away, and let him loose on everyone?"

Voss held up his wrist. CaLarca glared at the beads, the exposed string between them. "What of it?" she snapped at him.

"The beads," Voss explained. "I didn't know, until he went
to your farm."

"What are you talking about?" CaLarca demanded, her voice
pitching higher.

"They're weapons." Voss gazed at the beads, letting out a
long sigh. "When he activates it, granules multiply with heat
and spread in miniscule jumps, giving the appearance of a slow,
smoldering burn. I thought they were just a gift, but he took a
bead when he needed to make something disappear. It's what he
left at your farm, I believe. I'm sorry about that."

The bead that Phaira had tossed at her, and CaLarca had
thrown back in frustration, she remembered. A clue all along,
and she had dismissed it.

"I know that I can't take back what's happened," Voss continued." But -"

"You can do something now," CaLarca interrupted. "Teach
me to use Nyx."

Voss shook his head.

"Don't refuse me, Voss!"

"I won't," Voss said. "That was just a demonstration, to warn you about the power that you're up against."

"Liar!"

"Kuri and Shantou are dead because of his experimentations and control," Voss shot back. "They were twisted beyond recognition, and then the genetic and cybernetic manipulation - they were screaming inside."

"They weren't strong enough," CaLarca said. "I am, and you know it. I heard your thoughts. You thought I should be included in that original training group."

"That's not the solution!"

"It's better than holing myself away in some old border checkpoint, too afraid to show my face," CaLarca snapped. "It's better than hiding in Midland and mind-wiping Sydel again and again, like Yann did. Had I known Joran was alive, and causing all this destruction, I would have done something, I would have come out of hiding."

"If I show you, and he finds out, he'll use you as a weapon, like he did them," Voss pleaded. "You don't know how powerful Joran is."

"So what if he does?" CaLarca countered. "If I offer myself as a test subject in exchange for Ganasan and Bennet, then he can do as he likes. At least they'll be safe."

Voss was staring at her. CaLarca scowled at him. "Joran was always fascinated with me, right? He was the one who brought me into this mess. I can entice him to make the trade. I know I can."

Voss was silent. CaLarca lifted her chin. "Where is he?"

"I don't know if he's there now," Voss said, his voice shaking. "But your family is being held in Galee; it's a deserted factory, on the border of South and Midland. We've - he's had a few bases of operation over the years. It's guarded heavily, though."

"You got away," she pointed out.

"No one stopped me." There was disappointment in his voice. It made CaLarca want to smack him.

"Fine," CaLarca said instead, as her mind turned with ideas. She glanced at the narrow window up high on the wall. The wind was dying down, the storm was passing. "I need to make a call first. Stay here and don't move, don't talk to anyone. You're going to show me how to activate Nyx."

* * *

Outside, CaLarca made her way to the *Arazura*. The ship was crusted over with sand, the blue-gray metal only visible in parts. Renzo would be devastated to see all the little scratches on the paneling, she bemoaned. Using her sleeve, she brushed some areas clean, searching for the entry latch to bring down the stairs.

CaLarca.

CaLarca froze at the voice in her head.

Sydel. It couldn't be. She was hundreds of kilometers away.

It's possible. You're faint, but I can hear you.

"Sydel." she said the girl's name out loud.

You betrayed us.

"It was not personal," CaLarca said, trying to keep her voice even. "If I could have, I would have never incapacitated you."

You hurt the people I care for.

Here, a rush of guilt. Had she gone too far in rendering them unconscious? Was Renzo all right?

They thought you to be their friend. As did I.

"Are you coming for me?" she challenged.

There was no answer.

"I have no regrets, Sydel," CaLarca kept talking, her words growing tighter. "Everything I've done, it's been for my family. You wouldn't understand -"

And she closed her mouth, immediately regretting her words. Sydel never knew her family. Yann had manipulated her memory since Sydel became a teenager, removing almost seven years of her life, forcing her to rebuild herself, her abilities, her strengths again and again, to render her less powerful. Her mother was dead, and her father was a monster.

I won't forget this. None of us ever will.

The Eko connection broke, and CaLarca was left in silence.

Perhaps Joran's theory was valid. Maybe people like Sydel, like CaLarca, like any NINE, maybe they needed to be controlled for their own good. Because they would inevitable hurt.

Then Voss appeared next to her, looking the *Arazura* up and down. "Extraordinary. Where did you get this?"

"I told you to stay," she growled at him.

"I've been underground enough," he told her. "The ship?"

"I borrowed it," CaLarca said, doing her best to keep her voice steady. "It's not to keep." She banged on the side of the *Arazura*, so more sheaths of sand fell to the ground. There was the handle. She jerked it open, and more sand poured out, caught in the frame. She coughed and waved her hand to clear it away.

"Who do you need to speak to?" Voss asked, peering up the stairs into the cabin.

CaLarca grimaced. "Someone who can make this rescue a success."

VI

Back inside the *Arazura* cockpit, CaLarca stared at the console for several minutes, mustering up the nerve to input the connection code. She couldn't tremble or lose her temper. She had no idea what reaction she might witness, but she felt certain it was the only way to save her family.

Finally, she punched in the cc, and pulled on one of her braids to center her thoughts as it rang and rang.

The screen unzipped, and there he was: Theron Sava, in a suit, leaning back in a chair like a lord. He looked meaner, and older, in the week since she had spoken to him last. Had it really only been a week?

"Why are you calling me?" came his deep, bitter voice through the sound system.

"I have information for you," CaLarca said. "Valuable information. And I need a favor."

Theron snorted. "You want a favor from me."

"Yes. We have worked together before, and now I want to do it again."

"You want to work with me," he repeated, in that same smirky tone.

It was time to get to the point. "You had an advisor named Bianco Sava, correct? Who worked for both you and your grandfather? He's not who he says he is."

Oddly, Theron didn't look surprised by the news. "All right. Let's hear it. And how much is this going to cost me?"

"As I said," CaLarca reminded him. "I want to make a deal. I don't want any rana."

"Say what you want to share, and then I'll decide."

"Fine." She swallowed her nerves. "Bianco Sava is a false name. His true identity is Joran Asanto."

Theron grew still. "Joran Asanto," he repeated. "Of the Asanto Foundation, the multi-million rana trust. Joran Asanto died in Kings Canyon."

"He didn't," CaLarca said. "He's the one who brought the NINE together in the first place. And he is responsible for what happened to your family, and to mine, and to Shantou. All of it."

"You speak about him in the present tense."

"Because I have it on good authority that he's alive and faked his death."

"Whose authority?"

"That's not relevant."

"Oh really? How do I know you're not trying to manipulate me, like you do everyone else?"

CaLarca bristled. "Because my family is in danger," she spat. "And I have neither the access nor the means to get them out."

"You're calling me from the *Arazura*. Where are the others?"

"I need an answer, Theron."

"Why not ask your dear friends for their help? Unless, of course, you've already betrayed them. Again. I assume that's the case, if you're reaching out to me, of all people. Are you a thief, as well as a manipulator?"

"If you assist in the rescue of my family," CaLarca stated, "I'll protect you from Joran's NINE abilities. Then do as you like with him, as long as he ends up dead. That's the deal."

"Where is he now?"

"If you agree, I'll tell you where to find him. But not before."

Theron stared at her through the screen, his features so vivid that she could almost believe they were in the same room.

"I'll be in touch," was his final response.

Then the screen went black.

* * *

The box dropped in front of CaLarca with a thunk.

"You kept paper files on all of us?" CaLarca asked, looking up at Voss. "All this time?"

"I copied what I could from Joran's," he confessed, settling down next to her. "I wanted protection, an incentive to leave me alone, just in case. I couldn't trust anything digital, too easy to erase. I haven't loved him in years," he added.

"Years," CaLarca said flatly. "Can't imagine what it took to break the spell."

Voss looked pained at the remark, but CaLarca refused to take it back. She opened the box and flipped through the files.

Tehmi's was minimal, of course. And there wasn't one for Voss, no surprise there.

Shantou and Kuri's were the thickest: arrest records for narcotic possession, stolen vehicles, mug shots of the two of them, growing older and thinner and more sallow.

"He took advantage of their addictions," Voss explained. "They always needed rana, so they did assignments for him. Every time they got away, he reeled them back in."

I turned to the factory to drown out my memories, she thought. *They turned to drugs. I understand, better than I would ever admit. Who knows what I would have done, had I not gone with Ganasan and taken his offer?*

Now they were buried together in the Mac skerries: Kuri's bloodless corpse crushed under the collapsed house, Shantou's wrecked, mechanical body sunken into the mud.

"Joran was the one who changed Shantou into that red atrocity?" CaLarca asked.

"When he sent Kuri to find you, Joran promised to care for Shantou. But she wasn't well, mentally, and she let him experiment on her, growth hormones, brainwashing, cybernetic enhancements, all to see how it impacted her NINE ability. That's when I made the decision that I had to leave. I couldn't take the screams."

CaLarca was growing more disgusted with Voss by the minute. "So, you left her to be experimented on, because you couldn't handle it?"

Voss shrugged. "I never said I was a brave man, or even a good one."

Marette's file was thicker, with several press releases about her rise in music popularity as the performer EM LEE: interviews, curious scribbles in an unknown hand. "Shantou never went to her sister?" CaLarca asked, flipping through the records. "She must have seen Marette in the public sphere, known where she was."

Voss shook his head. "Marette paid for rehabilitation a few times for Shantou, begging her to get Kuri out of her life. It never stuck. After a while, they just stopped speaking. Shantou never mentioned her again. I don't know if Marette ever tried."

Yann's file was curiously bare. It didn't seem like they bothered much with reconnaissance for Yann, though perhaps it was due to the location of Jala Communia, so remote in the Midlands, and the fact that he was unmoving for the twenty-five years. There were blurry images, some jotted-down notes, but very little until she reached the end of the file and caught a photo of someone walking by Yann's side, shot from far away: Sydel, with her former braids wound on top of her head.

Then there were the last files, bundled together: hers, and Ganasan's. She flinched at the old photos of him, of herself, ten and fourteen years old, fierce and terrified in the flash. Yes, Joran had kept track of every stop she made, every factory she worked in in the North. They'd followed her to Ganasan's farm in the South. They had a picture of her with a pregnant belly, walking through the fields.

"I was lost for two weeks," she said slowly. "Lost between the time I went to Kings to find Sydel, and when the family found me in that crevice with broken legs. I don't know what happened in between." She lifted her eyes to Voss. "Do you know?"

Voss's gaze shifted.

"Don't bother lying to me," CaLarca reminded him.

"I don't know what happened, exactly," Voss said. "But I know Joran, Kuri and Shantou were gone for that amount of time, and that you were present, with them. I only heard short messages now and again, but no one would tell me what occurred. If I knew, I would tell you."

CaLarca stared down at the files in her lap. "I'm having trouble believing that one man could be the cause of so much pain and suffering."

"His one weakness has always been a hunger to see how much he can control. Everything was an endless experiment. Even our relationship."

"You need to stop mooning over him," CaLarca instructed. "It's getting annoying." She snapped the file shut. "Tell me how he got involved with the Savas."

"He stalked the children," Voss said. "He learned their contacts, and their routines. Then he actively put on weight, and changed his name, and waited for an opportunity. There was an assassination attempt on the former head of the syndicate, Iyo Sava. Joran was there, watching. He used Nyx on the assailant, stopping him from pulling the trigger. Then he stepped out and attacked, breaking the man's neck. Iyo Sava was grateful and offered him a position in his family as an enforcer.

"And over the years, he made himself indispensable to the family; he was able to make impossible deals, and calm agitation. Joran started to travel on Iyo's behalf to make negotiations and new partnerships, all with great success. Then he took the vows and took the Sava name as his own. That gave him access to the children, the four little cousins from Kings. Iyo Sava was their grandfather, their last living relative and now guardian. The children were teenagers, though, and growing wild. Joran reported on the four Sava cousins to Iyo regularly, advising on how to handle them."

"And what were you doing in the meantime, while all this was going on?"

"I took care of the compounds he established before his death," Voss said. "I cared for Kuri and Shantou when they showed up. I kept reading, and researching, and gathering information. I pretended to be the good spouse whenever Joran showed up. But I've been subverting Joran's schemes for some time now. It's why it's taken so long for him to even get to this point. I can at least say that I delayed the end of the world for as long as I could."

She wondered about Voss. His acute loneliness, of a life passed by, and nothing to show for it. In love with a monster for decades, and left with nothing but regret.

"I need rest," she told him. "I'm going back onto the *Arazura*. Don't follow me."

* * *

On entry, there was a blinking red light on the *Arazura's* console. CaLarca took in a deep breath and held it as she connected the audio.

"Three days."

CaLarca blinked. "Three days for what?"

"You give me the coordinates. Be there in three days, at this same time. And be ready to do whatever I tell you to do."

Fingers shaking, CaLarca entered in the location of the Galee compound, that Voss had mentioned. The information was transmitted. "What is your strategy?" she asked.

"You don't need to know the details. Just be there to receive the package when I deliver it."

CaLarca bristled. "My family is not a package, Theron."

"Do you want them out, or not?

"I want a guarantee," CaLarca warned, "that my family will not be hurt. Whatever you do to Joran, my family comes first, and their safety. Is that understood?"

"Joran, first," came his curious, distracted response. "Then everything after."

A tight sensation started in her chest. "Please just tell me the plan, what - ?"

"You don't get to set the rules, CaLarca."

"You can't just - "

"I can, because you need me."

She did need him. But she didn't like the tone of his voice. Theron was different somehow, from the man who stayed on the *Arazura*, who battled Shantou as the Red monster. Something had changed.

But what choice did she have?

"Agreed," she said. "Three days. I'll be there."

PART TWO

I.

Her face was cold.

Opening her eyes, the world rolled into view. Empty horizon. Sun peeking through the clouds. Sand and rock, with a thin sheen of rainwater.

Her dress was soaked, and the air was frigid.

Rolling slowly to a seat, Sydel had to drop her head between her knees. Her temples throbbed with pain. Her lungs were scraped raw. Her heart was skittering, its beat uneven. She could only imagine how the siblings would feel when they woke.

One by one, she crawled over to Cohen, Renzo and Phaira, who were sprawled across the ground. She placed her hand on Cohen's jaw, thankful for the brief warmth. She fixed Renzo's glasses so they were level on his nose. She smoothed the wet hairs from Phaira's face, and tucked them behind her ears, noting all the pale scars on the woman's face and arms. All three of the siblings had the same look on their faces, a grimace, as if caught in a bad dream. Best to wait and let them awaken naturally.

Cohen was the first, gasping. "What happened? Where are we?" he burst out, before he rolled over and retched.

Then Renzo's eyes shot open. He didn't move, just blinked. Then he craned his neck, searching the landscape, the lines in his forehead heavy. He was searching for the *Arazura*, of course, his treasure, his investment. Their home.

"I'm sorry, Renzo," Sydel said.

Renzo dropped his head with a thump. "And I taught her how to fly the damn thing," he muttered.

"She did this to us," Cohen said between choking breaths. "She left us. Threw us out like we were garbage."

Sydel turned her attention to Phaira, who was still prone on the ground. A drop of water tracked down Phaira's cheek. But it wasn't raining any longer, and the rest of her face was dry. It was a tear.

"Phaira," Sydel whispered. "Are you in pain?"

Phaira inhaled, a strange, shuddering inhale. Worried, Sydel opened her mind, just a little. Yes, Phaira was in pain, but there was no blood, no red threads for her to pull free. Phaira was surrounded by a strange brown-green energy, like she was sinking into mud. What did CaLarca do to Phaira? Was this her last bit of revenge?

Then a shadow cast over her, and Cohen was shaking Phaira hard on the shoulder. "Phair!"

Sydel went to hiss at him to stop, but Phaira's eyes flew open, her gray-green irises bright. "How long?" she croaked.

"Six hours," Renzo said, huffing. "She just left us here. Anything could have happened to us while we were unconscious. Someone, or something, could have..."

Then his eyes went wide, and he pulled out his Lissome from his pocket, his fingers moving in the air. Then with a yell, he threw the Lissome at the ground. It hit a jutting rock and broke apart from the impact.

"Rana's gone," he choked out. "All of it. She went into our account and cleaned us out."

"You gave her access to our account?" Phaira exclaimed, now up on one elbow, the palm of her other hand wiping at her face.

"I didn't think she'd rob us!" Renzo sputtered. "We were alone on the *Arazura* for over a month - we had to get supplies."

For the first time, Sydel saw how dangerous their situation was. They had no rana, no water, and there was no sign of civilization in any direction. And by the look of Renzo's Lissome, it was broken from his hurling it in fury; a tiny piece had been chipped off by the motion, which he now tried to put back together.

"Does anyone have another Lissome?" Renzo demanded, looking sheepish as he knocked the tiny flat square again and again.

Cohen was scanning the sky.

"Can you see something?" Sydel asked him, shivering.

"Smoke," Cohen said, pointing.

It was faint, and almost the same color of the clouds, but he was right: there was a thin stream of smoke. People.

"We need water," she reminded him, even more aware of how dry her throat was.

Cohen took off his rain-soaked shirt and coiled it like a spring. Then he wrung it over his mouth, and water ran down his chin. Sydel gagged, even though she knew it was foolish. She tried to find a section of her skirt that wasn't too dirty. Then she braced herself, ripped it clean and wrung a precious few drops of water into her mouth. There was a slight pool on the ground, in the crevice of a rock; she used the swatch of fabric to soak it up and braced against the taste of moss and minerals.

As she drank, a glint caught her eye, something black and thin on the ground. A sword, she realized, the one Phaira had used. She picked it up, wiping the mud from its brocade surface, surprised at how light it was.

"Our best option is to go north," Cohen announced to the group, wiping the back of his hand across his mouth. "If there's a burning fire, someone who started it has to be nearby. Maybe it's a village. At the very least, it might be someone with some idea of where we are."

"And if not?" Renzo pressed. "Maybe we should just stay here, try and get a signal."

Cohen cast a look at Sydel, and she heard his voice in her head: *Help me. Get them to listen.*

He was right. They had to stay together, remain calm, and find safety. She had to stop the reeling in her head, the temptation to collapse, to just accept that everything and everyone that they had counted on was gone.

Clutching the sword and sheath in one hand, Sydel extended her hand to Phaira. "Come on," she said gently. "We have to go."

Phaira didn't seem to hear. Still, Sydel managed to get the woman to her feet, even though Phaira was eight inches taller and far heavier, and prodded her to move. Phaira kept her head low, her blue hair covering her face. But she moved, and eventually Renzo did too, grumbling and scurrying behind Cohen as he led the pack, striding in the direction of the smoke.

* * *

Even with the smoke in sight, night began to fall as they walked through the plains, and Sydel started to wonder if it was really possible that they might die out in the middle of nowhere.

Finally, it was too dark to see more than four feet ahead. Cohen found a cavern for shelter. They gathered sticks, like they were kids at camp, and Cohen sparked a fire with stone. Then the four of them rustled into the space, and Cohen drew his arms around Sydel, warm and strong and comforting.

"We need each other's body warmth," he instructed his brother and sister. "So hug it out."

Phaira and Renzo made similar faces of disgust.

"I'm serious," Cohen growled. "I know what I'm talking about. Get close."

After some shifting and repositioning, Renzo and Phaira were stacked against each other: Phaira cradling Renzo from behind. Her arms were around his chest, and her sharp chin dug in his shoulder.

Renzo jerked away. "Stop that."

She gave him a smack on the arm in response. Renzo slumped heavily into her, making her squawk.

From behind, Sydel heard Cohen's sigh of exasperation. She cradled his thick forearm across her chest in her hands, and felt thankful, for once, that she was an only child.

The night was long. Sydel must have fallen asleep a dozen times, jerking awake, and seeing nothing but orange embers. Her feet and hands were numb. Even Renzo and Phaira had stopped fighting and were wrapped in each other's arms, huddled against the cavern wall.

The fire wavered all night, threatening to go out with every burst of wind. Then finally, finally, the black sky turned to navy, and then to purple, and Sydel wanted to cry with relief at the sight of the sun coming up. They had made it through the night.

Stomachs growling, throats dry, Sydel and the others continued to walk in the direction of the smoke, new bursts hovering in the sky. The landscape was changing, moving from flat and marshy, to rolling green and grey; were they approaching the mountain range? Were they coming close to Toomba, where Cohen's grandmother lived? Then Sydel did some calculations, on where they had left, and where they had been abandoned. Toomba was hundreds of kilometers away, to the north. She had no idea what was in this part of Osha, near the east and south border.

With difficulty they crested the first escarpment: Cohen holding onto Sydel's hand and helping her through the rocks, Phaira picking her way through like she had done it a million times before, Renzo stumbling and swearing every few seconds. Finally, they reached the top, and peered over the edge on the other side. All four gasped at the sight below.

Nestled in the shadow and protection of the valley were thousands of tiny red wooden huts, spread across the land, like a vast carpet over the vibrant kelly green. In the center of the spread, there were a few larger buildings, also in red brick, and there were the shapes of temples to the west, on the outskirt of one corner of the sprawl. It was startlingly beautiful, and utterly quiet.

"What is this place?" Renzo asked, panting from the effort of climbing.

Suddenly, Sydel knew. "It's a Jala settlement. Yann told me about this arm. It's the largest Jala settlement in Osha. People travel from all over to study here." What was it called? She wracked her brain but couldn't come up with the name.

Phaira's voice was faint. "We can't go down there."

"We don't have a choice," Cohen said gruffly.

"Cohen's right," Renzo coughed. "Just keep quiet and let me do the talking."

Surprisingly, Phaira didn't argue with her older brother. So Sydel tucked the sword into her waist sash, and slid her arms through Cohen and Phaira's elbows, both so similar in a way. Together, with Renzo in the lead, they made their way down the steep ridge.

The huts drew into focus. Different shades of red, she realized, some were crimson, or fire-orange, or faded pink. And the structures weren't next to each other, like she thought from above, but staggered, creating great, broken waves up and down the valley walls.

Movement at the entrance, the mouth of a dirt path, leading into the center of the town. People were gathering, men and women, both young and old, and of every skin color. They all wore loose trousers and tunics, but some bore sticks, and bos, and blades, while others were barehanded, with visible veins in their strong forearms. Sydel felt the muscles in Cohen's arm tense.

Renzo raised his hands in the air. "Please," he called out. "We mean no harm. We just need shelter."

The crowd murmured amongst themselves. Weapons were held tighter in fists.

Renzo looked over his shoulder at Phaira, his expression pleading for her to step forward, to show some intimidation, or authority.

But Phaira's eyes were unfocused, and her shoulders curved forward, her muscles slack.

Sydel was dumbfounded. What had CaLarca done to the woman?

Sydel gathered her strength and called out: "I'm one of you. A Jala, from Midland. My master was Yann Qin. Do you have a leader here?"

The crowd just looked at her.

"We beg of you, give us sanctuary," Sydel tried. "In the name of the faith - "

"They need to fight."

A voice hovered above the crowd.

Heads nodded in response. A few shouted to be chosen as opponents.

"Fight? We're not here to fight," Renzo burst out. "Didn't you hear what she said?"

"Show us what you know!" a woman called out.

Sydel searched for the source of both outbursts, but the crowd was pressing forward, and Sydel could hear the blood rushing in her ears.

Then her memory hit: this place was Soares Valley, where every resident was a martial artist, and in turn a teacher within the community. Their Jala path was pursuing ultimate perfection in physical and mental expression. They lived here, they practiced with each other, they fought each other in the open, and practiced their faith. And just like any other Jala community, outsiders were not to be trusted, but to be initiated into the flock.

"Wait!" she cried. "We accept! We will fight!"

The crowd stopped. Renzo and Cohen stared at her, both with hands in the air, ready to defend against the mob. Phaira's eyes were on the ground, like she hadn't even noticed the situation.

Sydel couldn't fight, of course. But the Soares people didn't know that, and they had to play along with what they wanted.

"We will fight," she repeated, her voice trembling, "in seven days."

"Seven days?" Renzo squawked, but Sydel ignored him and kept talking. "My group – my family - we ask for seven days before we engage in combat and attempt to gain entrance into your communia."

"What are you doing?" Cohen hissed under his breath.

"And in the meantime," Sydel continued. "You give us sanctuary, until a decision is rendered."

A faint grumbling came from the crowd, but Sydel knew there was no counterargument. Jala rules were the same everywhere, regardless of specialization. And the restrictions were the same, too, she knew: within the initiation period, there was to be no outside contact, and no leaving the borders, not without severe repercussions. That rule, they would end up breaking, Sydel knew, but the prospect of warmth, shelter and food overtook any future plans.

"Syd, we're not joining anything," Cohen was muttering, looking panicked. "What are you doing?"

A woman stepped forward, gesturing at the tower of houses. "Shelter east of the path is for women," she announced. "West is for men. Sexes only mingle at the academy, or at worship, or on this path for training."

Cohen snorted to himself. Sydel shot him a look.

Two men broke through the crowd, gesturing for Cohen and Renzo to follow.

Then strong, calloused hands landed on Sydel's arms, guiding her in the other direction, and more hands were prodding Phaira, propelling the women to the east side of the dirt path. No one spoke. As a group, they passed hut after hut, and finally one of the huts, orange-red in color, had an open teal door.

Inside, it was a simple shack; four walls, a firepit surrounded with a metal shield of some kind, and two beds on the ground, flat futons with heavy quilts, with neatly-folded bundles of clothing on each. Two women went to start a fire, and the others helped Sydel and Phaira to remove their dirty, damp clothing. Sydel clung to her body, embarrassed by the nudity, but Phaira had no response. Their old clothes were tossed out the door, and the new ones unwrapped: trousers and tunic bundles, in some kind of soft, jewel-blue material. Another body ducked through the door, into the hut, bearing a metal platter piled with rice, vegetables, some unknown form of meat, and a jug of water. It was placed on the mattress on the right, nearest to Sydel.

Then the women left, as silent as they came.

Phaira and Sydel were alone. The fire crackled. Sydel realized that she'd forgotten to take a breath during this whole process, and sucked in the smell of the hut: ashes, and wet earth, and smoke.

"Come eat, Phaira," she said, sitting next the heavy platter, and resisting the impulse to lift and tip the contents into her mouth. "Come and sit. It will be okay."

Phaira sank onto the other bed. Slowly, she pulled her legs underneath the quilt. Then she turned to the wall, so all Sydel could see was matted blue hair.

Night fell, but Sydel couldn't sleep. Her thoughts went in circles, tighter and tighter until she couldn't resist; she closed her eyes, and let her Eko go, let it soar in all directions, searching for that presence. Nothing, nothing, just other bodies, hands, deaths, skins, desert and rock and sand and urban waste, and pressure, mounting pressure, so hard that it made it hard to breathe, and....

And there.

There she was, flickering in the forefront of Sydel's mind.

CaLarca.

No, she could hear the whisper of CaLarca's thoughts. *It's not possible. Sydel.*

It's possible, Sydel sent down the chain. *You're faint, but I can hear you. You betrayed us.*

It was not personal, came CaLarca's response, higher pitched than normal. *If I could have, I would have never incapacitated you....*

Sydel grit her teeth. *You hurt the people I care for. They thought you to be their friend. As did I.*

Are you coming for me?

Sydel didn't know what to say. Her emotions were swirling so hard, she felt like she might burn a hole in the mattress and fall through to the floor.

CaLarca's words came down the Eko channel like waves. *I have no regrets, Sydel. Everything I've done, it's been for my family. You wouldn't understand.*

Tears formed in Sydel's eyes, angry, frustrated tears, and something else under her nose.

She touched her nostril. It came back dark.

She had to disconnect. It was all too much.

She sent her final message to CaLarca, before the darkness overcame her. *I won't forget this. None of us ever will.*

II

S ydel woke with a start. Even bundled under quilts, the tip of her nose was frozen.

The other bed in the hut was empty.

Sydel sat up, fighting the wave of dizziness that followed, and felt her heart skip a beat. The altitude, she reasoned, waiting for her body to calm. When it did, she swung her bare feet to the dirt floor.

Outside, the view of the valley was spectacular. Threads of yellow lights snaked paths through the settlement, illuminating the night. With so much light, Sydel almost missed the spark of orange on the roof below. Then she smelled the smoke.

"Phaira, don't."

The ember wavered.

Sydel's eyes were adjusting to the night, and she could make out Phaira's silhouette, huddled on the red roof. Soon, Sydel could see the twisted cigarette in between Phaira's second and third fingers, smoldering.

Where had she gotten the mekaline?

"Come back inside," Sydel said, shivering and walking closer. The smell of the smoke was overwhelming. "Talk to me. Tell me what's going on."

"I can't." She could barely make out Phaira's voice, but she did hear the crack in the woman's words.

"Why? Why can't you?" Sydel asked, inching closer, her bare toes gripping the red tile, until she stood at Phaira's side.

Phaira shook her head. "I can't. I just need to forget or - I don't know what... "

Sydel snatched the mekaline out of Phaira's hands and threw it over the rooftops.

"Phaira," Sydel snapped. "Whatever it is, it's not worth breaking your sobriety."

Anger spread across Phaira's face like a horrible mask, and for a moment Sydel thought that Phaira might punch her.

Thankfully, no blows were thrown. Phaira was breathing hard through her nose, but the anger was fading.

Sydel exhaled with relief. "Come on," she ordered. "It's freezing out here."

She reached down and took hold of Phaira's hand. "Your hands are so cold," she told her, giving her wrist a pull. "Come on."

Phaira didn't resist, but rose to her feet, and let herself be led back into the hut.

As they entered, Sydel leapt back into her bed, shivering and thankful for the thick quilts. But Phaira remained in the center of the room, still and silent.

"Phaira, come into bed."

Phaira's head swiveled. Sydel could make out her glittering eyes in the dark.

Sydel lifted the edge of the quilt, waving her in. "Come on," she said gently. "I'm cold too."

After a long silence, Phaira did as she was told. The weight on the mattress shifted, and the two women faced each other, both heads on pillows. So close to Phaira, Sydel felt a strange, strong affection for the woman: how she was so powerful, but radiated vulnerability in that bed.

"Syd?" came Phaira's whisper. "Do my brothers know? About him and me?"

Him. She was talking about Theron Sava. Was that why Phaira was so distressed?

Sydel hesitated. She thought back to the *Arazura*, when CaLarca had made rude comments to Cohen about the observed relationship between Phaira and Theron. Had Cohen believed the story?

"No," she finally whispered back. "I don't think anyone knows."

"You know."

"I guessed at it. It wasn't obvious."

"I'm so embarrassed."

"Why?"

"Because I was wrong. About everything."

"What did he do?"

Phaira said nothing. But in the quiet that followed, it struck Sydel that this was something sisters might do, this kind of intimate confessions late at night.

No more words were spoken, so Sydel did her best to comfort Phaira, stroking her arm, pulling the quilts higher over her shoulders. *I wish that she could have experienced some kind of happiness. Something other than death and violence and negativity. I wish for so many things for her.*

Anger simmered in her belly when she thought of Theron Sava, for making Phaira feel like this. After everything Phaira had done for him! After Sydel had healed him, and helped to bring down the Red.

How terrible, she thought, *after going through so much trauma, for them not to have a moment of peace.*

Who will be the one to care for you, Phaira? Sydel wondered, as she watched Phaira drift into sleep. *Who would you ever allow to do so?*

* * *

When morning light cut through the hut window, Sydel blinked awake.

What a pretty flower pattern on the pillowcase, she thought, still half-asleep. *Like a blooming rose.*

But no, wait. They were white pillows, she remembered from the previous day.

Sydel lifted her head to look.

It was blood, spread in a radial pattern. She'd had a nosebleed in the night. The stain was the size of Sydel's head. The side of her face had been sleeping in that. Horrified, Sydel flipped the pillow to the other side and rubbed at her face, searching for flakes of dried blood.

Sometime in the night, Phaira had returned to her own bed; her back was now to Sydel. Thank goodness.

Then Phaira turned, startling Sydel. "I'm sorry about last night," she announced. "It won't happen again."

"Oh, Phaira, stop it," Sydel couldn't help but retort. "Don't push it all down again. That's how you get into trouble."

Phaira lifted up on her forearm. Her dark mouth opened, like she was ready to argue. Then she deflated with a sigh, flopping down on the mattress.

Sydel sat up, praying that there were no traces of red on her face. "Why don't you tell me what happened?"

Phaira shook her head. "It's stupid."

"It's not stupid," Sydel corrected hotly. "It's not stupid to have feelings."

"You don't want to hear about it."

"I asked, didn't I?"

Phaira's jaw worked, like she was chewing on her words. Then she started to pick at the hem of the quilt, avoiding Sydel's gaze.

"He didn't want me," she finally mumbled.

"Then he's an idiot."

A smile quirked on Phaira's face at the declaration, and faded just as fast.

"But you were together," Sydel stated. "At some point."

Pick, pick went Phaira's fingers on the threads. "I don't really know what to call it."

"Do you love him?" Sydel tried, as carefully as she could ask such a personal question.

The response came after several long seconds of silence. "I thought I did."

Sydel stayed quiet, waiting for Phaira to continue.

"I have to hold parts of myself back with people," Phaira finally admitted with a lowered voice, like she couldn't believe she was confessing it. "All the time. But it felt like we understood each other. I could be weak, or blunt, or crazy, and it was okay. Though I'm probably wrong about that. I don't know."

Phaira glanced up at Sydel for the first time. "Is it like that with you and Cohen?"

Now it was Sydel's turn to flush. "I was weak from the start in front of Cohen."

"No, you got the best possible progression," Phaira corrected with a faint smile. "You might have seemed vulnerable when we first met, but look how much you've changed. No wonder he's crazy about you. He saw it from the start. The rest of us, it took a little longer."

There was another long pause. "I'm sorry things got weird last night."

"Phaira," Sydel said. "I've wanted nothing more than for you to trust me."

"I trust you," Phaira said gruffly. "Of course I trust you. Between Cohen changing into a mountain man, and Renzo being so secretive, you're turned out to be the only reliable one in the family."

The word struck Sydel. *Family.*

Phaira looked down at her hands. "But I don't know what to do," she admitted. "I don't know what to do, or where to start, or if I have the strength. Everything that's happened, it's been my fault. If I had refused Jetsun when she asked us to help. If I'd been nicer to CaLarca."

"To my knowledge," Sydel told her gently, "Renzo was the one who pushed for action against the Red. And Cohen and I came because we chose to. And CaLarca..." She let out a tiny breath, holding back her anger. "I should have known that she was about to explode. I should have been able to protect you all. So we have both made mistakes."

Both women regarded each other in the dawning light. There was a sense of relief in the air, and truth, and reassurance.

It will be okay, Sydel told herself, trying not to think of the bloody side of her pillow, still hidden from view. *It will all be okay.*

* * *

When Sydel was able to stand upright, she and Phaira dressed and headed outside to explore. A thousand red roofs, descending and rising with the valley, greeted them. Around every corner, in every open space on the dirty path, the residents were fighting. No, not fighting, Sydel realized, they were training with each other. Sparring, they called it. Some with bare fists, some with sticks. Dust clouds rose up and down the path, as footwork changed, and steps were taken forwards and backwards.

A village of warriors. Sydel had never seen anything like it.

And neither had Phaira, by the look of her wide eyes: how they darted, taking in the activity, and the slight flush of her cheek. There was a spark in Phaira, the first seen in days.

An idea struck Sydel. "You should jump in."

Phaira glanced over.

"Go challenge someone," Sydel said, nodding at the scene before them. "Go get that black sword, and challenge that guy with the wooden one, maybe."

Phaira let out a short laugh. "I'm not doing that."

"Of course you can."

"I meant, I'm not using the katana," Phaira corrected, a new, sullen tone to her voice. "It doesn't belong to me."

"Does that matter? You're skilled with it." Sydel caught Phaira's eye. "Go fight. It'll be good for you."

Phaira grimaced. "You're so bossy. I thought you were a pacifist."

"Stop arguing. You know you want to."

When Phaira descended to the dirt path, the pairings ceased to move. Silence fell across the valley.

Quickly, a makeshift circle formed around Phaira and her opponent, a slim black-haired man with dark skin, shirtless and bare-footed, his abdominal muscles prominent. No one cheered or hooted as they took position as observers; they all watched with the same interested look on their faces. This was a serious society, Sydel realized. They were there to learn, not to hurt each other.

Phaira rolled the sleeves of the tunic up each arm. Then she removed her shoes. When she stood upright, the man opposite put fist to hand, and bowed. Phaira mirrored the movement. Then each combatant settled into stances.

Sydel was fascinated. She'd only seen glimpses of Phaira in battle, or the aftermath of her injuries. This man with no shirt, they were roughly the same height, and size; that must be why they were pitted against each other. But what would happen?

The man was quick and in constant motion, bobbing and re-treating, lashing with quick punches and flicking kicks. Phaira was different, her shoulders rolled and settled, and Sydel could see that her breathing rate slowed, her motions stilled, watching the man. There was a different energy around Phaira, not that muckish green-brown, but something orange, and building. Then the orange burst, and the two were on the ground. Phaira was on top of the man, rotating and wrenching his arm, hyper-extending the elbow, as he frantically patted the dirt with his other hand.

It was over? Just like that?

What would the reaction be?

A loud bark of laughter. Sydel jumped at the sound, but it came from Phaira, who was smiling, helping her opponent to his feet. The man was nodding, and also laughing, brushing the dirt from her back.

The sound of three hard claps echoed through the valley.

Sydel started. The noise came from the surrounding circle, the watching residents.

She remembered the Jala ritual: when accepting a new member, the unified group gave three sharp handclaps in unison. The one time she participated in a welcoming ceremony, back in Midland, she was instructed to clap so hard, to create the sharp, staccato sound, that her hands burned for the rest of the day. But that was after days of demonstration and deliberation, weighing on the seriousness of bringing in another body to the fold. There had been so many meetings, and arguments, she remembered. These Soares Valley residents had decided to welcome Phaira into their fold without even a conversation. Why would they do that? Why were they so quick to accept Phaira?

Her confusion eased at the sight before her. As the last clap faded, Sydel watched from above as the circle moved in to embrace Phaira and shake her hand. Phaira, in the center of it all, couldn't stop the grin from spreading across her face. There was such joy, and respect, and warmth in the moment; it wasn't somber and serious, like the initiation Sydel remembered in Midland, with little words and no celebration.

Maybe this was how Jala was supposed to be. Maybe the fact that her time in Midland felt like a dream, a story about someone else, maybe that was a blessing. Maybe both she and Phaira were meant to find Soares, for Phaira to find acceptance, and for Sydel to find truth.

So many paths, she thought, *that I never thought I would take. So many more that I want to follow.* There was a strange, sinking sensation in her chest at the thought. She wondered why, watching as Phaira took on another opponent, a tall, muscular woman this time, and everyone else paired off, and Phaira was lost in the sea of rainbow tunics, one of many students, practicing under the sun.

W here's Phaira?" Cohen asked. "Why are you walking on your own?"

The brothers were also dressed in the local attire, tunic and trousers, and both itched at their right arms as they approached. Their faces were still drawn, with circles under their eyes, but they had eaten and gotten some rest, at least. Sydel, on the other hand, was more exhausted with every step on the dirt path that traced the circumference of the valley, past rows and rows of red huts, and the curious, empty temple in its center. The brothers had seen her, shouted out to her, and bounded out the door when she passed. They were situated so far from her and Phaira, she realized, nearly the length of the valley. Why so far?

"She's fine," Sydel said, with a touch of irritation. "But she needs time to herself."

"Why?" Renzo pressed.

"Because she does," Sydel said, feeling like a mother scolding her children.

Renzo and Cohen frowned, showing their blood relation in the way their chins grew sharper as their mouths turned down.

Sydel changed the subject. "Have you found a way to communicate with the outside?"

"Not yet," Renzo huffed. "No one has Lissomes here. There's barely even any electricity. But they have to have something, somewhere."

"They may not," Sydel said. "They seem self-contained. Perhaps there's never been a need."

"Come on, there's one Lissome, somewhere around here," Renzo scoffed. "There's no such thing as being self-contained. They have to leave sometime for supplies. Or order them. They've probably got a Lissome hidden in that main temple. I just have to get inside and find it."

"So what, then?" Cohen asked. "We break in? Or Syd, you were a Jala, maybe they will let you in and you can scope the place."

"I don't want to be deceitful," Sydel said. "They took us in and gave us shelter. I want to be respectful."

"It's not a terrible thing to want to contact someone," Renzo snapped. "We're not talking about killing someone or stealing things. If we get kicked out, so what, we'll have a ride incoming anyways. It doesn't matter if the people here are offended. We'll never see them again."

Sydel bristled with anger. Did he have no morals, or any sense of what other people might need, or want?

"Who are we gonna call?" Cohen asked Renzo, ignoring Sydel. "Anandi?"

"I don't think so," Renzo muttered. "She's pretty mad at me. At us."

"The detective, then," Cohen said. "Oz, whatever her name was."

"Actually," Renzo said, "I was thinking of calling Theron."

Sydel froze, half from surprise, half from the sudden anger in her.

"Man, I don't know," Cohen was saying. "Things got so crazy there, he's probably wanting to keep his distance, now that the Red's dead, and things are safe - never did get a thank-you or anything."

"It's different with him and me," Renzo said gruffly. "There's more to our relationship, beyond the Red."

Cohen frowned. "What, like you're involved or something?"

To Sydel's surprise, Renzo's face flushed. "No," he sputtered. "I just - we have some business to figure out..."

"What is it with this guy and everyone being in love with him?" Cohen nudged Sydel, making a face. "Do you like Theron Sava, too? Should I be worried?"

Sydel shook her head at him with wide eyes.

Cohen frowned. "What? Why are you doing that?"

"Wait, who else?" Renzo interrupted. "Not that I am - doesn't matter - who else?"

Cohen opened and closed his mouth a few times. Then he rubbed the back of his head, lifted one shoulder, and with a sheepish look on his face, said: "CaLarca said something about Theron and Phair. Like, doing stuff."

Sydel couldn't read the look on Renzo's face. She didn't dare to reach out and measure the emotions around him, so she could only guess at the thoughts in his head; some mix of jealousy, anger, revulsion, betrayal.

"That rat," she heard Renzo mutter. "This whole time? And you two knew about it? And you didn't tell me?"

Cohen lifted his hands. "I didn't even know if it was true!"

"You knew," Renzo addressed Sydel, bitterness in his voice. "I bet you knew."

Sydel lifted her chin. "It wasn't my place to say. It's not our business."

"Oh, it's my business," Renzo snapped. "This makes things complicated, and I don't need complications screwing up our plans, not when I'm investing my - "

"'Our plans,' meaning what?" Cohen shot back.

"Since everyone is so adept at keeping secrets from me," Renzo said snidely, "I think I've earned keeping one of my own."

He jabbed a thumb at the Soares temple. "I'm going in there, and I'm demanding a way to make a call, or I start causing problems. Are you coming, or not, Co?"

Cohen looked from Sydel to Renzo.

"I know," Sydel said quietly. "Go ahead."

Cohen shot her an apologetic look as he shuffled behind Renzo, making their way down the winding path.

* * *

When Sydel returned to her designated hut, Phaira was inside, in the center of the floor, kneeling on a cushion, her eyes closed, her head dropped, her index and thumb touching. Meditating. That was something that Sydel never thought she would see; Phaira calm, and quiet, and still. Watching from the doorway, Sydel wondered if she should leave. But fatigue dropped over her like a bucket of water. She needed to rest, and for that, she needed to interrupt.

"Phaira," she said softly.

"It's okay." Phaira looked over her shoulder. "Just trying to remember old habits." She shifted, winding her arms around her bent knees. "What's up?"

Another wave of fatigue came over Sydel, and for a moment, she felt on the edge of passing out. "I need to lie down," she announced.

"Go ahead."

With relief, Sydel went to the bed and collapsed on the mattress. Her heart was beating fast, and there was sweat on her upper lip. She closed her eyes and tried to speak evenly. "You seem better."

"I'm fine," she heard Phaira reply. "Having a break from everything, from reality, finally being able to talk to someone, it's been a relief. And I'm always better when I have a purpose. I think that fight woke something up in me. Time to get back into a routine, you know?"

"Maybe you're more of a Jala than you think," Sydel said. "Stronger with regimen and respect."

"Very poetic," Phaira said with a smile. "And probably true." She dug the ball of one bare foot into the floor. "That's something I miss about the military. I would have stayed there until retirement, if they'd let me."

A thought struck Sydel, and she turned her head to look at Phaira. "Did you ever think to join Osha patrol?"

"Who, me?" Phaira laughed. "Be serious."

"I wonder why you haven't thought of it before," Sydel said, with a growing curiosity. "You have a desire to do the right thing and protect the less fortunate. You have the physical means, certainly. You could be a real benefit to the community."

"I don't follow rules that well, Syd, remember?" Phaira reminded her. "Plus, I'm an addict, and a criminal. I've had bounty hunters after me. I've done illegal things."

"But you could teach the patrol so many things." Another idea struck. "As could I."

"What are you plotting at now?" Phaira groaned.

"I've thought this for a while now, Phaira. I want to show the world the good parts of NINE," Sydel said, lifting her head from the pillow. "Not just the parts to hurt people, or manipulate, or torture. The goodness of being NINE. People need to understand, it's not just horrible."

"No one is going to care about the good parts of being a NINE," Phaira told her. "It's only fear that resonates. Even if a few people accept you, more will want you dead."

Sydel sighed with frustration. Phaira was right, but Sydel didn't want it to be true. She wanted to believe in the acceptance of people. But the world wasn't as Sydel wished it would be.

"It's just a thought," she told Phaira. But it sounded funny to her ears. She couldn't make her lips form the shapes; it felt like they were being dragged down with hooks.

She repeated herself. A slur of vowels.

Phaira was scrambling to her feet.

Sydel tried to lift a hand, to tell her to stop, but her arm wouldn't stay aloft. It flopped back down to the bed. Weak. Numb.

"Syd!"

The mattress shifted; Phaira was shaking her shoulder, her gray-green eyes huge and terrified. Sydel looked into them, and caught the pattern of her own heart, so fast and skittering.

Finally, sensation began to return to her arm. With all her strength, Sydel scrambled to grab Phaira's sleeve. "Don't - tell - Cohen," she pushed out the words, finally intelligible.

"Don't tell him what?" Phaira demanded. "What just happened?"

"Need to breathe," Sydel said, shutting her eyes. "Need to rest."

But even with eyes closed, Sydel could feel Phaira's pulsing, anxious energy.

"Syd, why don't you want Cohen to know?"

Sydel took in several slow breaths, choosing her words carefully. "Because he will worry and take it too far, and I'm sure I just have a virus of some kind. I will go to the community healer for testing."

"What, here? What if they don't have one?"

"All Jala Communias have one," Sydel reassured. "As soon as I get my strength back, I'll go. I promise."

She opened her eyes. Above her, Phaira's dark mouth was tight, her brow deeply furrowed.

"Phaira. I promise."

Phaira dropped her gaze to the quilt.

In the moments that followed, Sydel wondered if Phaira might be picking up on Sydel's secret, racing thoughts.

This is no virus. This is no virus.

* * *

Inquiring down the path, Sydel learned that the Soares community healer was named Tomo, and after morning training, he could be found in the large temple in the center of the valley. To Sydel's great surprise, Tomo was the same man that Phaira had battled that morning. He still had dust in his hair, and some fresh bruises on his arms, but he nodded when Sydel explained that she'd had an episode of weakness and a nighttime nosebleed, and asked for him to assess her health. She barely felt the pinch of the syringe when he drew blood; they did have some technology here, she noted, for immediate blood analysis, and portable ultrasounds. That was encouraging.

Finally, after testing her from head to toe, Tomo surmised that Sydel had experienced a transient ischemic attack, a temporary drop in the blood supply to the brain, and the nosebleed was a release for her heightened blood pressure. He also had concerns about blood clots. Tomo recommended more testing and medication, and help outside of Jala Communia through a neurologist.

"But," Tomo added, looking worried. "The nearest specialist center is hundreds of kilometers away. I'm not sure what options are available - perhaps an airlift, but it would be at your cost... "

"Can we consult remotely?" Sydel asked, already exhausted from the visit. "I have a connection to a physician that I trust."

Tomo balked. "You'll have to secure transportation to meet with anyone on the outside."

Sydel glared at the man. "You are telling me," she said slowly, "that in times of medical crisis you still adhere to your no-contact rule?"

"It's the Jala rule."

"It's arbitrary," Sydel snapped. "And I challenge it. I want a Lissome, or its equivalent, for private consultation."

"I'm afraid that's not possible."

"Do you know who I am?" Sydel thundered, feeling a new rush of power. "If you did, you wouldn't want me dying on your watch, unless you relish the idea of widespread attention." As she spoke, she felt a tiny click of cold fear in her heart, so chilling that she put her hands to her breast, as if to warm her ribs from the outside.

She was going to die.

She could sense it.

It was coming, and she couldn't stop it.

The doctor's words broke through. "You cannot let anyone know that I have this."

"I won't," Sydel promised, without a pause. How easy the lies came to her now. She could remember a time when she was appalled at any form of deception. "Please leave."

Tomo shuffled out the space. Then Sydel entered a complex series of numbers and letters from memory, Anandi Ayjo's personalized cc that came with built-in encryption and firewall protection when it connected, something that Anandi had set up, long ago.

It took some time, but finally the callback came.

"You've got some nerve," came the angry girl's voice through the tinny speaker.

"Let me speak to your father, please."

"He's not available."

"Don't argue with me," Sydel said sharply. "This is between me and him. Do what I say."

There was silence on the line. Then, a succession of clicks.

"Sydel. Is everything alright?"

Sydel softened at the sound of her mentor's voice. "Emir. I need a consultation to confirm my findings. Though I'm not sure how to send you the information...."

Emir talked her through the transfer of information via Lissome, and Sydel did her best to follow.

There followed a long silence, and muttered exhales.

"Whose bloodwork is this?" was his first question.

"That's private."

"Sydel, please."

"I just need someone to confirm my findings, Emir."

A sigh floated through the Lissome speaker. "Well, blood pressure is dangerously high, for one thing. Circulation isn't great, heart rhythm is uneven. Evidence of damaged cells. How old is the person you're treating?"

"Fairly young," Sydel said.

"Well, if I had to go by these results, I'd say you're treating an eighty-year-old woman with some version of an autoimmune disease."

Sydel closed her eyes. So it was true. It wasn't just in her head.

"Sydel. Whose bloodwork is this?"

She felt the heat of tears between her eyelids.

"Tell me this isn't yours."

Even though she knew he couldn't see, Sydel shook her head.

"You need to see a hematologist."

"I'm far from any city," Sydel said. "And I don't have the rana to pay for treatment."

"I'll wire you the funds. I'll arrange for transportation."

"And when Anandi finds out what you did? That you're involved with us again?"

"I can function without her approval, Sydel. I'm her father."

"No," Sydel told him, gripping the Lissome in two hands. "I don't want to cause strife between you. Not when you've been given a second chance at life."

Second chance at life. The words resounded in her head.

"Then I'll come to you. I'll bring medications. We can talk about treatment options. I can run the tests again and make sure they're correct. At least we will know for certain, and it could buy you some time..."

Emir's words drifted into silence.

So strange, she thought. *I thought I might have a family one day.*

"I'm so sorry," Emir said, a strangled hitch to his voice. "If I'd known sooner, if I'd thought to even check for something other than your mental status... I never saw the need to check physically." The man was near tears, she could hear it.

"Thank you for everything," Sydel said quietly. "Thank you for treating me with such respect, and teaching me so much about medicine. I learned so much. And I enjoyed your company. I need time to think about my options. Please don't tell anyone about this."

And she disconnected the call.

"I'm keeping this," she told Tomo when he returned, closing the Lissome into its dormant form.

The healer opened his mouth to protest, but Sydel lifted a finger. "Not a word," she instructed. "To anyone about what you've seen, and what we have discussed."

"Answer one question for me, then," the doctor said, deflating. "Who are you?"

"I'm no one," Sydel said. "I never have been."

IV.

W hat's going on?" Phaira demanded, springing to her feet as soon as Sydel came through the hut door. "You've been gone all afternoon. Cohen was asking all kinds of questions, and I had to lie, tell him that you were meditating. What happened? What did the healer say?"

A warm flicker of affection grew in Sydel. *My friend,* she thought. *I don't want you looking at me with sad eyes. If this is the end for me, I want to make the decisions. Even if it means lying. Even if it means something worse in the end. Let them see me as I want to be: strong and confident, always ready to help. That's how I want to be remembered.*

Sydel smiled at Phaira. "Cohen worries too much. Just like I said, I've caught a virus, and I've overextended myself. I need to rest."

Then she lifted her right hand, showing the Lissome in her palm.

Phaira gasped. "Where did you get that? We can finally get out of this place! We need to tell Renzo and Cohen. Maybe we can get a connection to the *Arazura*, figure out where it is, if CaLarca still has it or not. If she does, I'm telling you, I won't be -"

"What about CaLarca?" It was Cohen interrupting, bending low to enter the hut, and eyeing both women.

Sydel sent an unspoken message to Phaira: *Say nothing.*

She heard Phaira's response: *Likewise.*

"We've got a Lissome, finally," Phaira announced. "Who would have thought it would be so difficult to find one? Where's Renzo?"

"I was hoping that he was here, with you," Cohen said grimly. "I haven't seen him since last night, and I've searched everywhere."

Sydel frowned. She reached out with her senses, trying to feel where the man might be in the valley.

There was nothing to hold onto. He wasn't in the vicinity.

Sydel walked to the window, staring out at the edge of the valley. The entrances weren't guarded, so he could have snuck out. But to where? Despite his state-of-the-art prosthesis, he couldn't walk for the hundreds of kilometers needed to reach a city.

Cohen's voice broke through. "What if he's in trouble?"

"He's not," Phaira said brusquely. "I bet he's with Anandi. Look, we'll call her now and she'll tell us, watch." She clicked open the Lissome and typed.

Sydel opened her mouth to protest. But she couldn't say anything without giving away her previous conversation with Emir. Hopefully, Anandi wouldn't mention anything.

A click, a buzz, and the audio-only light came on: "What do you want now?"

"It's Phaira. Is Renzo with you?"

"What? No. I haven't spoken to him in ages. Why, did you think he was?"

"We can't find him," Phaira said. "No note, nothing. It's not like him."

"No, that's more like you."

Phaira scowled at the Lissome. "What is it going to take for you to treat me like you used to? We were friends, Anandi. I always treated you - "

"You chose your path when you got involved with the Savas. You should have let that Red kill Theron. Now look what's happened. I might not like CaLarca much, but she didn't deserve to be assaulted like that - "

"Assaulted?" Sydel broke in. "What are you talking about?"

"You don't know?"

"We haven't had any access to technology," Phaira snapped. "If you cared enough to ask. CaLarca stole the *Arazura*, and we've been stuck in a village in the mountains."

Sydel heard the sound of rustlings, and clicks, a swooshing sound that she now recognized from Emir; a file had been transferred to the Lissome.

Then Anandi's bitter voice came through. "You all better figure out where you stand in all of this. Lines are being drawn."

The call disconnected.

And the video started: projected on the hut's stone wall, hazy with the sunlight outside, so everything looked muddy and blood-tinged. But Sydel could make out the outline of a towering gold building at the end of a long entryway. The video was shot through the latticework of black gates.

A deep, gruff voice came through, off-screen. "Hold this."

Phaira went very still. That was Theron Sava's voice, Sydel realized.

Then came CaLarca's pinched voice, retorting: "I'm coming with you."

"You're both staying here, and shielding my men," Theron shot back, still out of frame. "Remember the deal."

What had CaLarca done? Sydel could hear the whispers of another man, somewhere off-screen. Had CaLarca reunited with her husband and son, after all?

The video continued to roll.

Sounds of gunfire, distant and tinny. Footsteps. Short, quick breaths.

When Sydel squinted, she could see smoke coming out of the gold building, billowing through the door. The camera started to shake, but kept filming.

"He's not there," a whisper floated through, another man's voice. "He's not there."

"Quiet, Voss," CaLarca snapped. "Concentrate."

Voss. Sydel knew that name. She wracked her brain. One of the NINE, Sydel finally remembered. Zarek Voss. CaLarca was with him?

More rattling gunfire echoing from the house.

Then silhouettes appeared through the smoke at the door. Another shadow emerged, so tall his head almost hit the doorframe.

Theron Sava stalked down the path to the gates, carrying something small, and wiggling.

No, someone: a toddler boy, covered in dirt and blood, screaming.

The Lissome dropped to the ground, making Sydel wince with the loud jolt of feedback. But it continued to film, angled up enough to record the transfer; Theron dropping the child roughly into CaLarca's arms, her knees collapsing under the weight, the boy clawing at CaLarca's braids.

In the background, Sydel saw another silhouette emerge, stumbling closer: a man with grey-streaked hair, and hollow grooves in his cheeks.

"Ganasan!" came CaLarca's shriek.

In the corner of the frame, Sydel saw Theron's profile, dark with disgust. He was reaching into his pocket.

The Lissome shook, and CaLarca was screaming.

Then the video cut, and there was nothing but static.

Cohen was the first to break the silence. "I don't get it. Those two hate each other. And was that her partner and kid? The ones being dragged out?"

"Yes," Sydel said faintly.

"So, Theron sent in guys to save CaLarca's family," Cohen pieced together. "But then he did something to incapacitate them. Why would he do that?"

Sydel glanced at Phaira. The woman was muttering to herself, running her hands through her blue hair again and again. The energy in the hut was taut and vibrating.

No, not just in here, she realized. *Something's happening outside.*

She turned to the door, stretching out with her mind, dreading what she might see in the distance.

Something was approaching the valley.

She couldn't get a sense of who it was, but it was a mass of several bodies moving like a swarm, full of determination and aggression.

A strike of fear went through her. Maybe Theron Sava had sent his men to the valley, just as he had done on the video. Was he really so evil? She never thought that of him, but that video showed a different man than she remembered.

"Someone is coming," she announced to the others. "We need to go."

The sunlight was blinding. Cohen's warm hand pressed into the small of her back. Phaira's blue head and broad shoulders were in front of her, approaching the crowd that had gathered at the edge of the valley, a sea of scalps and loose hair and straight spines.

"Phaira Lore!"

Phaira skidded to a stop, so abrupt that Sydel ricocheted off the woman's back with a thump, and only stayed upright with Cohen's help.

Every head in the crowd turned to stare at them.

Then the residents began to part, stepping aside to create a long divide to the village gate, where a dark cluster of people waited.

PART THREE

I.

Under Anandi's direction, the hacktivist group turned super-collective, the Hitodama, had shifted its focus. Instead of individual searches for random information, Hitodama members were now focused on one thing: the Sava Syndicate; what it was doing; how they could stop what they were doing, and how could they dismantle it for good.

Hitodama members worked daily on a variety of tasks: scrambling communications; intercepting messages and shifting them slightly to cause confusion; taking inventory of all Sava-related businesses and persons in Osha; monitoring active bounty contracts; and, most importantly, tracking where Theron Sava was every day since that video was released of the Galee ambush. Anandi's Lissome was a near-constant buzz of information and pixels. The speed of the feedback often correlated to major activity happening within the Savas. But there was little information, unfortunately, when it came to Theron Sava. She caught glimmers of where he was, and who he was speaking to, but he was good at hiding his movements.

Leaning in her deep pink chair, Anandi flicked her finger to expand the pixelated picture she'd just been forwarded. That familiar dark head ducking under a door, his long black hair always tied back with red cord, like some stupid monk.

It was still surreal, equating the stories told with the boy she remembered as a child, when they were forced to 'play' together during family meetings. With such an age difference between the two, eight years at least, there was no shared interest. So instead, they just orbited each other, distracting themselves with books, eavesdropping (a mutual interest, it turned out), and peppering each other with uncomfortable, sometimes offensive questions, just to see who could make the other flinch. Theron was skinny and tall, even back then, with that straight black hair falling in his face, his features too big for his face, his eyes dyed to the golden Sava shade since the day he arrived at his grandfather's house. He was weirdly obsessive about certain things, movies, or characters in books, watching the same things again and again. She saw him teased relentlessly by his cousins, Keller, Xanto and Kadise; even though they were all the same age, they still treated him like a joke. And he took the abuse, always. Anandi couldn't remember a time when he ever fought back. Instead, she noted evidence of outbursts in the house, when she managed to break away and wander. A hole punched in the wall. A chair, legs broken, in the corner.

Theron even had a seizure once, in front of her, and it scared her so badly she almost wet herself. She had run over, pushed down his shoulders, tried to hold his head as it jerked back and forth, and hollered for help. Instead of rushing over, Anandi remembered how the adults' heads turned, and how their faces showed embarrassment, instead of panic. Eventually, the household staff came over, working with silent expertise to remove Theron from view, leaving Anandi on her knees, wondering what she just witnessed.

How strange, Anandi thought, swiveling in her chair, bringing up her legs to cross on the cushion. *How strange the way things turn out, how we have circled back to each other, but this time, each of us with power.* How odd that stealing secrets had led her to this point.

"I wish you'd share with me what you've found." Her father was fond of saying to her, when she had a moment to breathe, and he snuck up on her. "I can never tell what you're thinking anymore. You're so sad all the time."

No, Anandi thought, dissolving the image of Theron Sava in her mind. *Not sad, but not as carefree as I once was. Once pretended to be.* Everything in the past few months had sobered her positivity, to the point where she couldn't quite remember what it was to just laugh, without wondering who might overhear.

Maybe it was a part of growing up, something Anandi had been determined never to do. She wanted to be travelling, untethered, until her likely death at thirty (she could never picture herself past the age of thirty, for whatever reason). She turned down numerous job offers in her teenage years for that reason. She'd dragged her father all over Osha for that reason.

Now everything was different, since the Hitodama had come to Anandi for leadership, in the wake of the fears that shivered over Osha every day. The members of the Hitodama were all hungry for purpose, men and women, young and old alike, Anandi discovered. They all wanted to be productive, and hold true to their forward-thinking beliefs.

And what better representation project to disassemble than the archaic, outdated system that was the Sava Syndicate?

But being a leader did not come easily to Anandi. She spent many hours contemplating running away. Surely, there was someone more suited to this leadership position. She got drunk; she complained to whoever was still awake in her bed; she made threats to expose the Hitodama to the public; she made motions to smash every Lissome she owned, but always stopped before the final blow.

And when she could, Anandi stole away from visibility, looking for guidance in the most unlikely place she could have imagined.

By all accounts, she was the only visitor that Lander had anymore. Even the other Hitodama, the ones that Lander used to lead and command, they all steered clear. Was that her future, too? Forever replaceable?

"Before I bring him out," the nurse said, a new one, Anandi noted, with a suspicious eye, "I need to register you at the front desk."

Anandi unzipped the cargo-pants pocket on her thigh, and withdrew the passport, stamped with a blurry photo of a blue-haired woman, labeled as Mala, Ikani. In retrospect, she wondered why she ever thought she could pass for Phaira; all it would take is a concentrated look at the picture. But it was all she had, and she presented it to the nurse, who looked down with a frown and back again.

"Is there a problem?" Anandi asked.

"Not at all," the nurse said, handing back the passport. "Are you a relative, or a friend?"

"Relative." It was easier to say that. "I'm here every week."

"Sorry, I'm new," the nurse said, though her clipped tone didn't suggest an apology.

"Any updates?" Anandi asked. "The last time I was here, the doctor said that there were some improvements?"

"Well, his motor function was still a concern, and speech, but his brain activity seemed to be increasing in complexity. But he's taken a downturn, unfortunately. His behavior has grown erratic. I'm afraid that the doctor has chosen to postpone plans to release him at this time, until we determine what's gone wrong."

"That's sad to hear," Anandi said quietly.

The nurse handed back her passport. "I know. But please, enjoy your visit." The nurse gestured at her coworker, who was pushing Lander's wheelchair down the hallway.

"How are you, Lander?" Anandi called out, sliding the passport back into her pocket. "I hope you don't mind another visit from boring me."

Lander lolled his head at her, and smiled with only one half of his face. His hair had grown out, long and black and shaggy around his face. He'd grown thinner, too.

"How's that new nurse?" she asked when they were alone. "Treating you decent? Seems like a big pain."

One shoulder rose and fell. Lander's eyes narrowed at her, asking a question without saying a word: What are you doing here? There was a trace of old haughtiness in those piercing eyes, like he used to be, when she was playing pretend at being a Hitodama. How long ago that seemed.

"Not much has changed since last week," Anandi told him. "But we've managed to stop some shipments and scramble some communications. Everyone is working really hard. I just hope I'm doing the right thing. Telling them to do the right thing."

The shoulder lifted and fell again.

"You're right," Anandi agreed. "Who can say what's right? Everyone does terrible things, including me. There's a line that crosses somewhere. I wish it was clearer sometimes."

Lander was staring at her, his head shaking in tight little bursts.

"You're safe," Anandi soothed him. "No one is going to touch you."

"NINE," Lander spat the words.

"They aren't here," Anandi said, rubbing his arm. "They won't find you, I promise."

Lander's eyes grew round and afraid, and he clutched his arm, as if he were afraid that she might yank it off. "NINE," he repeated, shuddering.

"I know," Anandi agreed, resentment swirling in her chest. "NINE."

II

Travelling back to her base of operations, Anandi removed the passport again, and stared at the picture. Why had she held onto it, all this time? All it did was drudge up all her insecurities, all her memories of how she'd first gotten ensnared by Phaira and her brothers.

Ten years, ago, she, along with other mathematicians, had been recruited to help put an end to a small, but violent conflict in the West, their task to clear communications, satellites, and codes, so casualties could be minimized, and a treaty could be developed. Neither side was budging, and they were speaking in code to each other, so Osha asked for remote translators and codebreakers. It was a brief assignment, only seven days, but she always remembered the intensity of it. She was so young, only fourteen years old, and smarter than everyone in the room. If she volunteered, the university told her, they would clear her disciplinary record, and 'forget' about her violation of private records. It seemed like a simple choice, and another way to keep going. For Anandi, stealing information was natural. A slip of paper in her boot; a swipe of her Lissome to make copies; little secrets, little tells, here and there to gather and store away for another time.

So, she was in a cramped lab space, somewhere in the desert, with a bunch of men and women just as hot and frustrated as her, waiting for directions. And she'd overheard a conversation, looked over and seen a young man whispering furiously into a Lissome: "Do you have a shaved head??"

When she'd craned her neck to get a look at the visual, Anandi saw the face of a girl with gray-green eyes and sharp features. Her heart had fluttered at the sight.

The man, however, was red-faced, hissing into the Lissome: "You're too young. Just turn around and go home. There's a war going on, and you've just put yourself on the front lines. They could deploy you over here, and then what? We don't even know what - "

"Why are you mad at me?" came the girl's interruption, her voice dark and husky, despite her youth. "I'm of age. I can be useful. I've had training in martial arts, I'm strong, I pick things up fast. I can help - "

The audio cut off as the young man clicked his Lissome closed. Curious, Anandi watched him out of the corner of her eye, how tightly he gripped the mechanism, how his mouth moved without sound. She felt drawn to him, somehow. Everyone else on this team, they barely wanted to have anything to do with her, for her youth, for her genius, for her odd, awkward looks.

She rocked back and forth on her heels, waiting for him to notice her. Finally, he did, glaring at her over his glasses, his blond hair flopping over his forehead. "What?"

"That your girlfriend?"

He made a face. "My sister."

"So what's got you so upset?"

"She joined the army without telling me."

"Oh!" Anandi exclaimed, with growing interest. "Well, good for her."

"No, not good for her," the man shot back. "Reckless, and irresponsible, and done when I'm not at home to stop it, of course. The one time I'm not there...."

"Geez, you sound like her father."

"Someone's got to be in charge, and it ended up being me."

"Well, she won't get deployed," Anandi reasoned. "Training for the first two years, minimum."

"And if the conflict continues out here?" he shot back.

"This isn't a war," she reminded him. "It's a skirmish that people want to bury." She eyed him up and down. "You really hate being here. Where do you study?"

"Daro. Experimental mathematics."

"You wish you were back there?"

There was a curious shift in his expression. "Here, it just seems we are sitting around, waiting to be useful," he finally said.

"I don't wait to be useful," Anandi said.

The young man stared at her. "What's your name? How old are you?"

"Ani," she said. "And old enough."

One side of his mouth quirked in a smile. "Well, I'm Renzo. You kind of remind me of my sister. Does that mean I have to watch out for you, too?"

Smiling back at him, Anandi made a decision.

I'm going to find out everything I can about you and that sister.

And she kept to her vow. Since their dismissal from the conflict one week later, she had been somewhat stalking Renzo and

Phaira for the past ten years, never interacting, never interfering, but keeping track on their whereabouts. She checked once a week to see if anything had changed. Through her dogged schedule, Anandi knew every detail of the siblings' lives, available on the network and deep within official files: their genetic codes, their medical records, their arguments with child protective services. She debated, time and again, about getting in touch with Renzo, trying to resume a friendship, but each attempt made her feel foolish. She was notorious by then as Anandi Ajyo, known hacker-cracker, along with her father. Though she never told her father about her tracking. She never told anyone.

And now, at the other end: bitterness. That was the primary emotion when it came to the Byrne family. Bitterness, for involving Anandi in their complicated, near criminal dealings. Too many times, they relied on her and her fast-moving fingers and her endless paths of intel, without thought or care to the consequences to her. She was just a computer for them. She wondered sometimes if they even liked her as a person, or just saw her for how she was useful. Bitterness, resentment, and nostalgia, sometimes, for that brief moment in time that she and Renzo built the *Arazura*. When she taught him hacking and cracking. When Phaira protected her from law patrol's sudden attempt to arrest her. When Phaira held her hand when Anandi's father was near-death, and she couldn't cry any more tears.

Then, once again, the Savas had ruined everything. Turned the family to their side, poisoned them into thinking they were doing good. It made Anandi sick to see the reports, detailing the appearances of Theron Sava, with the Byrne family at his side. Theron Sava had become a threat the moment his grandfather died, and he was the only blood successor. Phaira and Renzo were fools to not realize it, to not heed Anandi's warnings and run far, far away. They had chosen to believe a Sava over her.

It was her hurt, and her determination that led Anandi to discover the truth behind Bianco Sava's identity. In truth, she wondered why she hadn't made the connection earlier.

When the Sava killings started, and Anandi dug deeper into the underworld, she immediately took notice of the man who was always with Theron, the advisor's oddly-empty history beyond twenty years. Too similar to the NINE timeline, she thought on first glance. Some deeply-hidden image files, scrounged up from the strangely well-protected Asanto Foundation, confirmed her fears. He was fatter, older, and balder than he once was, but he had the same eyes, even though they were dyed gold; they were the same as Joran Asanto's. Incredible; he had leeched himself onto the grandfather Sava and taken a place in the family.

For what purpose, though? she wondered. The Asanto name was still relevant. Why build another legacy?

Because that's what Bianco Sava had been doing all this time, it seemed, as she waded through recorded conversations, travel plans, surveillance files from every corner of Osha, showing Bianco Sava speaking with noted syndicate members, shaking hands, exchanging funds. He was making deals across the continent. And given the secrecy of these dealings, Anandi suspected that it wasn't for the benefit of the syndicate.

A report came in, from one of the Hitodama monitors: *I think I found the Arazura,* came the scrolling text. *It's been impounded in Ivo: abandoned, supposedly. Registered to a rental company, but it has the same blue paneling that you mentioned. Do you want to claim it?*

That was curious. Anandi has been unable to track the *Arazura,* since learning CaLarca had stolen it. That was surprising; it was usually easy to pinpoint the ship and peek into the family's affairs. Now here it was: stolen, likely shoved into some awful warehouse, waiting for a claim within seven days before it was torn apart for scrap metal. She knew how things worked in poor towns; there was a lot of rana in the *Arazura,* and its parts could be useful to someone. She'd had a part in building the thing, she'd assembled all the engineers to work under Renzo to make him feel useful, stubborn and prickly as he was. Did she ever even get a thank you? She couldn't remember.

Still, something tugged at her. This wasn't right, as hostile as she felt about the Byrne family. Renzo adored the *Arazura.* She could remember him sitting on its roof in that hanger, when they were building, running his hands over the paneling, how comfortable he was in the pilot's seat.

How many times was she going to go through the motions of saving them? If it wasn't for her, they would have been dead or jailed months ago. She could just send someone to claim the *Arazura,* so it didn't get junked. That was favor enough.

Anandi leaned back in her chair, stomping one foot on the ground. No. She needed to go herself. An honest exchange, for once in her life. No corrupted files, no masks. Visual confirmation that the beautiful ship wasn't destroyed. Maybe she would take it for herself. Long past-due payment for everything she had done for that family.

** *

"You can't be seen in public. I'll go."

Anandi sighed. "No one knows what I look like, Papa."

"Do you know how many times your name is mentioned in a day, Anandi? You might not tell your father what you're doing, but your actions make big ripples."

"You don't have to stay," she told her father. "I'm wondering why you are still following me around, if I'm honest. You don't need blood transfusions anymore. You don't want to get involved in Hitodama, anyways. Maybe you should go back to work somewhere."

Emir looked pale and startled. "I want to help you," he corrected. "As your employee, or your friend. Or yes, even your father."

In that moment, Anandi thought of Phaira: was this what she felt like, always pushing people away who sought to be involved? It was lonely, and terrifying, but the right thing to do. What a feeling to process.

"I just think it would be better if we were to separate, and talk later," she told her father. "When things have calmed down. After I bring back the *Arazura*."

"You haven't flown a ship in years."

"I can manage."

"You won't go alone, though."

"Papa," she said firmly. "I'll make that choice myself."

Emir looked at her for a long while. Then he spoke: "You feel like I've betrayed you, don't you. When Sydel came to work with me, and I supported her going to Theron Sava's aid. You haven't been right since the day that happened."

He was correct. Still, she worked to keep her anger out of her voice. "You knew this was going to happen, eventually. And you sped up the process by getting involved. Theron would still be laid up if it wasn't for Sydel, or any of them. He might even be dead. Then I could focus on something else, rather than constantly thwarting whatever horrible thing he is planning."

Emir had no answer. In watching him, she saw him as old for the first time, the white in his beard, the slump of his shoulders, the fatigue in his eyes. Her chest panged at the pain. He was tired. They were all so tired of this.

This was why she stayed with the Hitodama, she reasoned. So fathers and daughters never fought about such things. That they were never drafted into service on account of their names.

That people like Theron Sava were never allowed to develop.

* * *

Despite the fight with her father, Anandi chose to bring two Hitodama with her, each with some experience with physical matters. Anytime she ever tried to fight, she was clumsy, and completely ineffective; her brain was her weapon, not her body. But Quinlan and Pero had access to firearms. Pero even knew some martial arts, he told her proudly. Between the three of them, they could get a hold of one impounded ship.

As twilight made the gentle shift into night, the three got off the train, and made their way to Ivo. Through the chain link fence, Anandi could see stacks of old ships and transports, abandoned and crushed. Her heart gave a little flip, hoping they weren't too late.

On approach, she could make out a silhouette, standing at the possession booth, speaking with the attendant.

Someone extraordinarily tall.

Anandi's lungs seized, and she pulled on Quinlan and Pero's arms so suddenly that they both squawked with surprise.

"Quiet," she ordered.

Then the shadow stepped into the light, and she saw the telltale black hair, tied back with red cord: Theron Sava, speaking quietly to the attendant.

"He's here," she whispered. "Why is he here?"

Her heart thudded in her chest as Theron walked into the impound lot. Anandi gestured for the others to follow the perimeter of the chain-link fence, trying to move quickly and quietly, and achieving neither, plump, short, clumsy thing that she was.

When they rounded a corner, Theron was standing in front of the *Arazura*, hands in trouser pockets, looking up at the silent, looming mass. It was dirty, far dirtier than Renzo had ever left it. Still, it was majestic, if a little broken-down in appearance. He didn't move from his spot. Curious.... Theron was alone?

She had to run. She had to say something. Maybe she was the only one who dared to.

"Stay here," she ordered Pero and Quinlan. "Whatever you do, don't come out."

There was a small tear in the fence, and as the two held the hole open, Anandi gingerly stepped through, wincing as an edge caught her arm. She crept closer, and closer, as Theron lifted a hand, as if to caress the blue paneling of the *Arazura*.

"Don't touch it." Her shrill voice rang through the yard.

His gloved hand hovered.

"You have no claim to it," Anandi challenged, scurrying to his side.

Theron turned his head, so his profile showed. His tone was amused as he responded: "Neither do you. And yet here we both are."

"For Renzo," she shot back, craning her neck to glare at him, wishing for the thousandth time that she had a few more inches to her frame. Her hands were fists at her sides, and for a brief flash, she wondered if she would do any damage at all if she punched him in the face.

"Same as me," Theron said wryly. "Not the first time I've served as a delivery boy for that family."

Anandi went still. "You're – you're getting the *Arazura* for Renzo? Is he with you?"

"Funny to see you," Theron continued, as if he hadn't heard her question. "Because I've been meaning to make contact. I could use your -"

"No," she shot back. "Answer my question."

Theron raised an eyebrow. "I didn't even say - "

"I don't care. Why did Renzo leave his family in that valley and go with you?" she pressed. "For what purpose? What have you roped him into, Theron? Isn't it bad enough that you already recruited Cohen and Phaira?"

"Anandi," Theron broke in. "We have history, so out of respect, I'm keeping my hands in my pockets. But guard your tone with me. People are listening."

Who do you think you are? she wanted to scream at him. *I knew you when you were skinny and ugly and a joke among your own family.*

But her own eyes went to his pockets, and she could only imagine what he might have concealed in there, what he could pull out in an instant and slice her in half with. He could click his fingers and wipe out the Hitodama, truthfully, those people that she had come to care about.

"I'm extending an invitation for you to join me in Lea." His eyes flickered over her head, glancing at something. "Well, not so much of an invitation. You know how it is."

A cold shiver went over her skin. "Don't do this, Theron."

Instinctively, she looked back over her shoulder, searching for Pero and Quinlan. There was no sign of her friends.

"Too late," came Theron's detached voice, as the canvas bag went over her head.

Cold circled her wrists, and she couldn't see, or barely breathe, with the hands on her yanking, and pulling, her shoes scraping on the ground. She cried out with fear, and then she heard it - the sound of firearms in the distance, and then more shots fired, so loud they felt like they were right by her ear. She shrieked and squirmed, trying to wrestle away. But she could only hear and feel; Theron's hot fingers around her upper arm; the sound of the *Arazura's* hatch opening with a rusty groan;

the groans and whimpers of Quinlan and Pero, somewhere in the distance; the clang of her feet on the metal floor.

Then the air shifted, and they were in an enclosed space, she could sense it, and Anandi was shoved backwards, falling into a cushioned chair. She felt the fabric of the bag pulsing against her open mouth as she gasped for breath, and writhed, and finally went still when she felt the engines rumbling under her feet.

Only then did tears start to fall, desperate and terrified, and all she could think about was her father, and how worried he would be when she didn't return.

Time passed. Anandi made an attempt to dry her face with her shoulder through the canvas bag. Theron was in front of her, somewhere; she could hear his even breath, and the squeak of his gloved hands. Gentle beeping. The rush of air. The near-soundless engines under her feet.

She was in the cockpit of the *Arazura*.

Anandi swept her foot in front of her, feeling for the edge of a hidden compartment that she knew Renzo installed in the cockpit for smuggling. There were weapons in there, and other inventions. Maybe if Theron was distracted, and if she could get her wrists free? She'd never fired a gun, or hurt anyone in fact, but maybe she could figure out a way to subdue Theron.

And fly the *Arazura*? With him in it?

Her foot went still. No, it wasn't possible. She had to wait until they landed, until she surmised what his plan was. All she needed was a Lissome, to contact the Hitodama and give the call to attack. Hers was still in her front pocket. Theron hadn't removed it, strangely enough. Occasionally, she heard him mutter under his breath, little whispers that sounded full of worry, or resentment.

Then Theron's voice grew louder, making Anandi jump. "Cohen, Sydel and Phaira - they're still in that valley?"

"I don't know where they are now, and I don't care." She twisted in her seat, trying to find some give in her arm bonds.

"What's your problem with them?"

Help me, her thoughts begged. *Save me.*

She heard Theron give a soft chuckle. "You know, I have my own issues with that family. I might be sympathetic to yours."

"Take the bag off and I'll tell you," she challenged.

With a whisk, light flooded into Anandi's eyes, and she screwed her eyes shut to adjust them, embarrassed at the sweat on her face and the state of her hair. When her vision cleared, she saw Theron glance at her, and then turn back to face the pilot controls, gazing through the windshield. Did she catch a look of shame in his face? She couldn't be sure with her eyesight so blurry. She took in gulps of fresh breath and tried to gather her thoughts.

"So?" came his detached voice. "Your turn. Why are you mad at them?"

Anandi stared at the back of his head. He was still pushing it?

He was in need of someone to commiserate with, she realized. She could serve that role. He was practically begging for a confidante.

If I can make him think I'm on his side, he'll relax his guard enough for me to break loose.

It was the best chance she had. She couldn't see the coordinates to where they were flying, and the sky showed nothing but blue.

"Because - because I'm tired of being a convenient computer for whoever calls begging for help," Anandi started, thinking quickly. "With no regard to how it impacts me, or my father. I've never gotten a thank you, or any invitation to be more than just a disconnected voice for their one-time use, and I'm sick of it. I'm more than that. I'm capable of more than that, and I'm worth more than that."

"That's not a reason." Theron's response was a huff.

Anandi balked. "You said you were sympathetic."

Theron glanced over his shoulder, his profile dark and hawkish. "She saved you and your father from jail, twice now, if I'm correct, once in Honorwell and once in Liera. She was arrested in your place and was willing to go to prison instead of giving you two up. Everything she did, she did to protect you two, and her family, and that was the only -"

His sentence stopped.

"I don't want to talk about Phaira," he added gruffly.

"You brought her up," Anandi shot back. "I meant the lot of them, not just her."

Though she couldn't see the motions, Anandi heard the sound of fingers tapping the flight controls. It all came together for her, in that moment, and she cursed herself for not having realized it earlier. He and Phaira. Their familiarity in Honorwell, how they bickered under the balcony when helping Anandi and her father to escape. The fact that Phaira got out of patrol custody in the aftermath, with nothing to her record. It was him. They were involved, and probably for longer than she knew. He knew about Liera; how could he know about that unless he was there? Was he the reason why Phaira was sneaking out at night? Anandi felt both sick and furious at the thought. In another time and place, she would have been jealous. Anandi had never been sure if Phaira was straight or gay or some combination, she always seemed so aloof. Does she even have any feelings? Anandi had wondered time and again, as her resentment took root over the last few months. But this was different. This was some kind of connection that she hadn't even realized, even with all her eyes and ears and access.

What is the right move? she wondered. *Should I talk about Phaira? Should I be derogatory towards her? Or defend her? What does he want to hear?*

"We're going to see Renzo, right?" she tried instead. She was still trying to figure out how they were connected. Why Renzo would leave his family behind and go with Theron? Theron had hired the family before for protection. Maybe this was an extended contract? "Is he working for you again?" she blurted out.

"Not for me, no," came his response. "A partnership."

Anandi held back her gasp. Renzo had joined ranks? He was a Sava?

Theron looked over his shoulder. "And one that you can be a part of, if you're open. I know you think I'm scum, but you might think differently if you see what I've been trying to do."

Anandi didn't know what to say. *Careful, careful,* her thoughts warned.

"My hands are bound, Theron," Anandi finally spoke. "This isn't really a situation that leaves me 'open' to new ideas or partnerships."

She saw a slight flush in his neck. "You're right. We'll be landing shortly, and I'll take them off. I'll need your Lissome though. I know you've got at least one on your body."

Reflexively, Anandi put her elbow over the tiny black square in her pocket. *There will be others,* her thoughts whispered. *Stay calm and keep him talking.*

"And don't be mouthy again when we get there," Theron added. "It's one thing in a junkyard, another when you're surrounded by my people. Don't cause someone to overreact. I don't need the mess."

Was that a threat, or a warning? Anandi stared at the back of his head.

Theron gave a soft *hmph*! of an exhale. "Funny, isn't it? Where we both ended up? You running the Hitodama, me the Syndicate. Always thought it would be Keller doing this, never me. Never thought I'd be here."

"Neither did I," she had to admit. "You know how much I wanted to be free of all of it. I didn't want to be an Ajyo, and everything it entails."

"I'm starting to think it's just fate," he muttered. "Doesn't matter what we do, or who we try not to be. It all would have happened, no matter what. I'm a Sava, you're an Ajyo. We play the same roles, again and again, one generation and the next."

Maybe that was true. She was an Ajyo, and he was a Sava, and their families had been in business and friendship for decades. A tiny part of herself accepted this, relaxed and ready for the role he was presenting. Their families, finally reunited.

It made her made her think of her father, and a rush of panic went through her. Had he been captured, too? What about her people? What if the Savas were slaughtering them all now, as she flew through the sky with hands bound? What if he was distracting her, easing her into a trap?

"Whatever we decide, Theron," she choked out. "My father remains free. I don't want him involved, not in any of this."

"He's never been a factor." That flat, dismissive tone was back in his voice.

"Does that translate to 'he's safe and unharmed'"? she couldn't help but press.

"Like I said," came his quiet reply. "He's never been a factor."

* * *

The windshield went dark and cold, and the engines quieted. It was so dark, Anandi couldn't see where they had landed. She forced herself to not squirm with nerves, even as Theron rose from the pilot's chair, unfolding to his great height and stretching his back.

He gestured at her. Warily, she stumbled to her feet, and waited.

She felt the brush of his hand on her wrists and heard a tiny click. The fasteners released and fell to the floor with a clang.

She rubbed her wrists and looked up at the giant man. He pulled his overcoat over his broad chest and buttoned it. "Come on," he repeated curtly, ducking under the doorframe, heading for the *Arazura's* exit hatch.

Outside, they emerged into a compound, so vast that it took Anandi by surprise. She flicked her gaze in all directions, searching for some kind of geographical marker. She looked up at the vast brick building, its crumbling exterior: red brick and stone, old windows, cracked glass, the whistling of wind through the roof. What was this place?

"Used to be a school for troubled youth," she heard Theron say. "When it was condemned, Grandfather picked it up. Now it's in my name. Thought it would be good to put the property to use."

For a school, there was a startling amount of security measures built into the area, as Anandi discovered when she followed Theron, taking note of the guards patrolling the area, the endless number of men and woman that moved on rotation, checkpoints, metal detectors.

On entry, Theron handed her a thin half-circle of metal. "Put this on," he instructed.

Anandi thought about arguing, but paused when she saw Theron put on his own loop, affixing it behind his ears, and under the long sheath of hair, so the silver glimmer was barely visible. Tentatively, she mimicked his movements, feeling its smoothness, the tiny impression in its center, where her fingertip hovered. She felt the tiniest click, and stiffened. But nothing happened.

Theron was looking down at her, a strange look of bemusement on his face. "It's protection," he told her. "You'll need it from them."

He gestured at a series of doors, three in total, with a slit of a window at the top.

From them?

Anandi looked through the first window on tip-toes.

She recognized the green braids immediately.

A toddler was asleep in CaLarca's arms, wrapped in a blanket, as she rocked back in forth in her kneeling position. She was staring at the wall. Anandi wondered if she should knock, or wave. Then a wave of shame went through her; what was she thinking?

Quickly, she glanced into the other two rooms. The middle cell held an older man with long hair, dark skin and heavy lines on his face. He was sitting cross-legged on his cot, playing with a bracelet of black stones. The room on the far side held yet another man, younger, thinner, bearded, who paced the width of the small space, and caught Anandi's eye when she looked in. The partner Ganasan, she realized, the one from the video. He was being kept apart from his wife and child. Why? And who was the man in the middle? Another NINE?

Fingers trembling, Anandi touched the loop of metal around the back of her head. "This is the HALO you made with Renzo."

"The improved version," Theron corrected. "Stronger, and more disruptive to NINE frequencies without sacrificing quality. There's been a lot of progress. Come and see."

Theron walked, heading down hallways, and Anandi scampered to follow, feeling like a mouse chasing a giant, the way he took such long strides. Amber eyes lowered as he passed, and lifted to stare at her. She was utterly confused now, between the HALOs and the apparent hostage situation that was taking place, even though she acutely remembered the video that spread across Osha, of Theron's men storming a building, and the violence that followed. Theron had gone through the trouble of freeing CaLarca's family, just to take her and her son into custody?

Anandi shivered and forced her legs to keep moving.

The hall opened up into what might have once been an auditorium, but the space was now filled with noise; whirring machinery, smelting and heat, the stench of chemicals. Piles of metal and tools, spotlights on various stations. And there, in the harsh florescent light of one, was Renzo Byrne, welder goggles pushed onto the top of his head, his regular glasses on his nose, his skin shining with sweat, and a look of pure bliss on his face. From a distance, Anandi stared at him, and wondered if she were to punch him, if he would fall, or just laugh at her.

"Ani!" came the surprised cry. Renzo slapped down his heavy gloves and came running, sweeping her into an embrace. "You're here!"

"Seems you had two people trying to get the *Arazura* back," she said through clenched teeth. "Coincidence."

Renzo's smile faded as he let her go. "I know this looks bad to you."

Anandi chortled. She put her hands on her hips, staring at Renzo. To her relief, his eyes were still gray-green, and not amber; if they had been, she didn't know what she would have done.

"But he's my business partner," Renzo corrected. "And with our inventions, we'll make sure that no one ever gets hurt by NINE again."

Her thoughts turned, putting pieces together. Since the *Arazura* was first built, Renzo hadn't stopped creating. He'd been working in a mad spree over the past few months: the HALO, the stealth technology on the *Arazura*, those SCKAFO leggings for CaLarca's legs. This was how Theron had snared him. Through invention.

Renzo took her by the wrist and steered her to where he was working. "Remember the electromagnetic pulse project that I came up with on the *Arazura*, that you activated in Toomba?

I came up with a smaller version some weeks ago, a Disruptor Coin."

He held out his hand, which held a simple coin-shaped piece of metal. "And I'm glad I did, because it was the only thing that stopped the Red from..."

He paused, his eyes clouding over.

Then Renzo continued. "I've made it even smaller, so it can slip into a pocket, and be activated by the edge of a fingernail. But the DC is strong enough that anyone within a ten-foot radius who is NINE will be impacted. It'll short-circuit their brains for a split second, just enough to disrupt whatever they're doing, so a person can get away, or call patrol.

"Then the HALOs," he kept on. "They should be standard in every vehicle, on every patrolman's belt. We have no idea how many NINE there are, Ani. Sure, CaLarca's group, but remember Huma, remember all those people she recruited - who else is out there? They're multiplying, and they can hurt people. It can't happen again. These people need to be managed. And if they're not willing to be public about what they can do, then we make it obvious."

Listening, there was a part of Anandi that agreed with what Renzo was saying. She had never liked CaLarca, and the woman had caused nothing but trouble and manipulations, but she couldn't help but feel bad at seeing her imprisoned and under guard.

"He's holding CaLarca prisoner," she said carefully. "And her family. You're ok with that?"

Renzo shrugged. "She made her choice."

Renzo was her closest friend. She knew more about him than anyone, and yet, when Anandi looked at him now, he looked so unpleasant. She never quite felt their age gap so strongly than she did in that moment.

"I'm not starting a war," Renzo said, as if he were reading her mind. "Nothing here is lethal. But this will prevent so much violence and suffering. It's necessary. Look at what they've done to my family. Huma and her brain scrambling. Kuri's manipulations, almost killing Cohen. Lander, stuck in an institution. Yann Qin, messing with Sydel's mind. The Red mass murders. All NINE, all corrupt. Not one of them has used their abilities for good."

She couldn't help but ask: "You think Sydel is evil?"

"Sydel isn't included in any of this," Renzo said brusquely. "She's a special case, and she'll always be separate, as long as she can keep herself under control."

Or else?

"Is this all for a specific buyer?" she pressed. "Someone who knows about the NINE?"

"No, it's for the public. That's where you come in, Ani. At least, I hope you'll agree to it." Renzo's eyes were intent on hers. "There are information embargos about NINE. The information has been held back for decades, and it should be public record. Osha needs to know about the NINE, and we're hoping that you might be the one to spread the word in a controlled way, so not to overwhelm the public."

Anandi felt faint.

"It's time, Ani. It's time people knew the truth, and that they are able to protect themselves. The three of us, working together? We can save hundreds of people from unnecessary harm. I know it's different, but if you think about it, you know it's the right thing to do."

This wasn't what Anandi was expecting: not devices to help people, to stop NINE from hurting others.

"I need water," she breathed. "I need a minute to think."

Theron's hand was around her elbow, then, and steering her away, out of the auditorium, into the murky hallways, filled with amber eyes watching. She let him lead her, trying to suck in as much oxygen as she could, to chase away the dizziness that threatened to overwhelm.

When she looked up again, they were in a new room. Once a classroom, but now a sanctuary, the room was closed off from the outside, outfitted with a desk, and a dozen Lissomes.

"A lot to take in," Theron said, not unkindly, gesturing at a chair. "Sit down."

"Yes." Anandi sank into the cushion and eyed the deactivated Lissomes on his desk. If she could slip one into her pocket, she could contact the Hitodama, and send out warnings, send out commands to everyone she knew to lock down, to destroy files, to shield identities, and get her father into custody. Alert the patrol to their presence, to what they planned to do....

Though, as she thought more about it, was there really anything for them to do about it?

Theron wasn't breaking the law, for once. Manufacturing wasn't illegal. The patrol didn't even know what NINE was, or what it was capable of doing. Look at the Kings Canyon massacre, and the covering-up of Em Lee's death in the Toomba

mountains, and even the Red itself. Even with so many wit-
nesses, it was still shrouded in secrecy.

Maybe they know more than we think?

*Or maybe they are just determined to keep the truth from the
public.*

The truth was Anandi dreaded the NINE as much as both
men did. After what happened to Renzo, to Phaira, to Lander,
how could she not see them as a threat? She feared CaLarca and
everything she represented, and even Sydel a little bit. The girl
was nice, but she was dangerous, and it had been a mistake, letting her get so close to Anandi's father. She should have watched
more closely. Sydel could have hurt Emir at any time, plumbed
his memories, controlled him at will. Anandi shouldn't have let
them be together without precautions.

And if she felt that way about her father, why shouldn't the
rest of the continent be informed, and protected, even if it came
through Sava means?

It felt easy, and logical, and it terrified her.

Is this how it started, going down this path of evil?

"Theron," she began, keeping her voice low. "You didn't
bring me here to spread gossip. I know you better than that.
What's your real need?"

Theron gave a faint smirk. "We don't know each other that
well, Anandi. By proximity, really."

"And yet, here I am, in the middle of your machine," she
pointed out. "You know what I can do, and I know what you're
capable of. You don't need me to spread information. You could
do that yourself, easily. So why am I really here?"

His fingertips drummed on the table, one quick succession of raps, before falling still.

"What aren't you telling Renzo?" she pressed. "You don't want to involve him in the Syndicate, do you? You can't want that. And you know he can't stick to just making trinkets, and not get involved in the rest of it. What happens when the two cross over?"

"It won't."

"Don't be stupid," Anandi growled. "I've lived with the shadow of your family for my entire life. It never goes away, and it never lets you go. Why would it start doing so now?"

A long pause. Then, finally, Theron spoke: "I have something for you."

He took the Lissome on the far right of the desk and slid it over to her with two fingers. Anandi resisted the urge to snatch it up and run. Instead, she eyed it with suspicion.

Theron chuckled. "It's not going to electrocute you. But it's locked, just so you know, so don't bother trying to open it. You won't be able to. Not until I activate it."

A sinking feeling in her stomach. "Then what am I supposed to do with it?"

"Keep it safe and hidden, until the right time." Theron got back to his feet, looming over her. "I have another request. Find Joran Asanto for me."

"You mean Bianco Sava?"

"I mean whatever form he's taken, I want to know where he is and how to find him."

"How does he fit into your little manufacturing plans?"

Theron's face darkened, and for a moment, Anandi thought he might hit her.

She tried to reason with him. "You don't need me for –"

"Find him," he interrupted, his voice like a bite. "Track him down, in any way you can. Any information you can steal. Any firewalls you can break. I want his exact location, where he sleeps, where he eats, and who is supporting him. Tap cc calls, or other correspondence."

"Why don't you do it?" she couldn't help but snipe back.

"Because I'm building a business." He swept his arm across the room, gesturing at the Lissomes. "I need an answer, and some kind of decision from you, Anandi. I'd rather it be of your free will, for it all to be, moving forward. I respect your talent, I always have. We've taken care of each other, I think, from a distance. I have, at least, for both you and your friends."

She couldn't say yes.

But she was in a compound filled with Savas.

She couldn't say no, either, not audibly.

But I can steal, came her thoughts. *And I can gather information. And I can sabotage from the inside. For whatever reason, he's a fool to bring me in this deep and expect me to behave. I'm surprised he hadn't mentioned all I've done to stop his correspondences and transactions.*

He's distracted. Getting sloppy. This is an opportunity.

"I'll find him," she told Theron. "If you meet my terms."

"What do you want?"

"I want my father off the radar."

Theron sighed. "Why are you so preoccupied with him? I have no use for Emir."

"I want to speak to CaLarca and her family," she tried. "Whatever details they can provide on where Joran might have ended up. What have they told you?"

"Nothing. They won't talk." Theron looked away. "I'm working on something to help with that, but it's not ready yet."

His gaze came back to her. "You go in guarded, though. Full HALO, with Disruptor Coin, and guards on them. She might try something."

"Fine. And last thing: I want access to everything." She wet her lips, pushing forward. "No supervision, no intimidation, no restrictions. If you want me to find Bianco, I need to understand every crack of the Syndicate, and who might be hiding him. No firewalls, no alarms. I get to look where I want."

"Done." Theron nodded at the Lissomes. "They're all actively connected. Look where you want."

Anandi stared. He couldn't be serious. Was he crazy, or desperate?

"But," he added. "These Lissomes are programmed to only provide information. You can't send out anything, no ccs, no messages. So if you had a hint of trying, don't bother. I'm going to choose to believe that you are a woman of your word, and are here to help. So thank you."

Theron ducked out of the room, and Anandi was left dumbfounded, staring at a dozen Lissomes, wondering what kind of parallel world she had been dumped into.

IV.

To Anandi's surprise, the other Savas treated her with respect, even calling her Ms. Ayjo. They brought her hot food with utensils. They offered her choice accommodations for bathing, for rest, assuring that they would stand guard outside her door. The family name, coming in handy again. She didn't know whether to be relieved or repelled.

The cameras installed in the abandoned school were open to her viewing, and she could see into each of the cells. Anandi saw the top of CaLarca's head, how she paced as her son was sleeping in the little cot, her braids swishing across her back. The man in the middle was called Voss, she figured out, though he barely moved, or interacted with any food slipped into his cell. In the third cell, she sometimes saw Theron in there with Ganasan, though there was no audio, and from the angle, she couldn't read lips. They would just sit in chairs, across from each other, and talk. No violence, no signs of an argument, though Ganasan's face remained cold and mostly still. Theron had the audio somewhere, she was certain. She wondered what they talked about.

When Anandi worked up the courage, she asked to see CaLarca.

It was just after noon. There were four escorts, heavily armed, shockrounds in one hand and Disruptor Coins in the other. Anandi felt the weight of the HALO on the back of her neck, and touched the chip, wondering if it was active, before stepping inside.

The cell was outfitted with anti-NINE technology, Theron had told her, more inventions from him and Renzo: ways to scramble thoughts, to stop projections, all things that sounded crazy, but in some ways fascinating. Renzo's brain was on fire, and he was constantly in that auditorium, sketching, welding, creating, and barely sleeping from what she could see. She saw the REM injector marks in the crook of his arm. The marks made her think of her father, and his need for blood transfusions, when he was still sick. She'd asked Theron to let her people know she was safe, and he promised to do so, but that was the only thing she had heard.

If anything, she thought, *Theron is a man of his word. I have to believe that, at least, until I figure out what to do. And what questions to ask. And what kind of a threat CaLarca is.*

Inside the cell, the green-haired woman seemed asleep. Her head was against the wall of the room, back in the corner. The toddler son was whining, picking at a meal pack. There were cots, and blankets, and a latrine, and a running faucet for water. It could be worse, she reasoned.

Anandi felt the weight of barrels behind her. Working to keep her hand steady, she unlocked the door, and pushed in it.

Inside, the woman had no reaction, yet her eyes were slightly open, and glazed. Is she communicating with someone? the thought occurred to Anandi. She looked all around, noting the wiring, the piping, the cameras. Was it possible, even with all of Theron's defenses?

Slowly, Anandi knelt to the floor, trying to catch CaLarca's eye. The young son saw her first, pointing at Anandi with a chubby hand, and scrambling next to his mother's side. The boy looked like CaLarca a little bit, with those black eyes, but his skin was warmer, and more golden, very different from her blue-tinged skin and green braids. Anandi wondered if he'd seen his father since coming here.

"Hello, CaLarca," she tried. "We've never seen each other in person, only on screen, but hopefully my voice sounds the same." Every word came out fawkward, and ridiculous.

"Are you okay?" she added. "Do you have enough food? Are you warm enough?"

Were these the right questions to ask someone who was being held captive?

The boy made a few incoherent noises. CaLarca's arm went round him, and he snuggled close. She still didn't look at Anandi though.

"We have a common goal, I think," Anandi began. "Finding Joran Asanto. I know you have a past with him, and he was holding your family hostage. Even faked their deaths, I guess. I'm so sorry that I was the one who told you they were dead... "

Her voice faltered, and Anandi felt shame creeping up her neck. "I know this isn't the most ideal of circumstances, but whatever you can tell me about Joran, or Bianco Sava, I can track him down."

And then what? she wondered. It wasn't as if she and Theron were going to be pals again. This was all so confusing. She didn't even know why she'd asked to talk to CaLarca in the first place, as a condition of her service.

"Who was the man in the video with you?" Anandi pushed. "Voss, I think? Is he one of the NINE? Is he a friend of yours?"

Nothing. The boy was looking at Anandi with curiosity, but CaLarca was a statue.

"You should have stayed loyal."

Anandi jumped at the sound of Theron's voice.

Theron leaned on the side of the doorframe, flanked by bodyguards.

Only then did CaLarca's gaze lift and focus on Theron. The tension in the room grew hot.

"That's the difference between you and me," CaLarca finally spoke, her voice dry and low. "I've always been loyal to the ones I love. I did what I had to do."

"That seems to be a common sentiment among NINE," Theron said. "Doing what's necessary, whether it hurts, or destroys, or kills."

CaLarca laughed, high and reedy, and utterly strange. "As if I didn't volunteer my life to protect yours. Or take down Shantou, after she murdered your cousin."

"You stole the *Arazura*, and left those – that family - for dead," he accused. "The ones who cared for you when you were lying half-dead in a mountain. You could have killed them."

"As you say, Theron," CaLarca sneered. "Loyalty, above all."

To Anandi's surprise, CaLarca started to rise to her feet. As Anandi backed away, she caught sight of CaLarca's leg braces, shimmering under the florescent light.

"Anything, and everything for them," the woman said, "I'm prepared to do."

Theron scoffed. "You can do nothing while you're in this building. You can't use any of your NINE abilities, not in this cell. I've made sure of it."

CaLarca's black eyes narrowed. "I don't need NINE to hurt you."

Suddenly, CaLarca grabbed a section of pipe that snaked up the wall. It came loose, to Anandi's surprise, with a *clank!* And CaLarca was attacking Theron, and the little boy was screaming, and the guards behind her were wavering, their barrels and shockrounds following their movements, around and around.

"Don't shoot," Anandi screeched at them. "Don't shoot her!"

Then her jaw dropped. Theron moved incredibly fast for such a large man, avoiding the swings. CaLarca hit the wall and sent the plaster crumbling. She caught Theron once, across the knee, and he wobbled for a half second, and barely missed her swipe, an inch from his mouth. Finally, he grabbed the pipe in one hand, the sound making a loud THUMP through the room and bore down all his weight. CaLarca was fighting back, but her knees were crumbling, and she was crying out in pain. Then he snatched the pipe out of CaLarca's hands and pushed her down hard.

CaLarca skidded across the floor, letting out a gasp. Then she snatched up the howling boy and huddled into the corner with him. The boy's screams had quieted to whimpers. CaLarca had her face turned away from the door, so all Anandi could see were her braids, hairs standing on end.

Anandi was hustled away, in silence, to her quarters. She went to bed, put the covers over her head, and replayed the scene again and again in her head: Theron's violence and his protection, CaLarca's savagery and helplessness. She wished desperately for someone to talk to. But there were no outgoing calls available, no way to drop a message without raising suspicion, and she didn't know yet where she stood, and how much she could risk with Renzo.

Patience. Patience.

Renzo came into the office where she worked the next day, holding two cups of tea. The steam brought back memories. *We shared tea when we build the Arazura together,* she thought, accepting the cup. *That seems so long ago. I never thought we'd come to this. Did he hear what happened yesterday? Does he even care what happens to CaLarca or her family?*

"How goes it?" Renzo asked, propping up his feet and sighing.

"Steady," Anandi said carefully. "And you?"

"Good." Renzo smiled as he took a sip. "You know me, I'm happiest when I'm working. It's a thrill to have so many resources at hand. We work well together, Theron and I. Who would have thought it? It feels good, though, that I'm playing a part in making the world a little safer."

"You know, Ren," Anandi began. "I do think people with NINE abilities are dangerous. And I can see the logic behind what you're building here."

Renzo flushed with pleasure.

"But," Anandi added, "I can't help but think that original NINE group? That was a special case. A select group, under stress, buried underground for weeks and experimented on. Maybe it was the environment that caused them to lash out, not the abilities themselves."

"Huma wasn't a part of it," Renzo pointed out. "Or her minions."

"That's true," Anandi admitted. "But still – "

"I don't think I really thought about it, or understood it, until the Red," Renzo continued, as if he hadn't heard her. "That was pure evil. Unfiltered desire to hurt and torture. The things the Red did..."

Anandi saw his hands tighten around his cup, and she wondered if he might crush the ceramic.

"Jetsun didn't deserve that," he continued. "She was a pain, but she didn't deserve that. It's not the environment, Ani. It's the wiring. Sooner or later, a NINE hurts someone. I don't know if they can help it. And what chance do people like you or I have, when they can reach into your mind, or manipulate your energy so they can throw you off a mountain? That's all I've seen so far. I haven't seen it ever used for anything good."

His words were true, Anandi had to admit it. She'd activated maps, and tracked people, but she'd never had her mind touched.

What did it feel like, she wondered, staring at the top of Renzo's head. *Did it hurt when Lander was taken? Did he have any memories of it?*

She couldn't forget that about CaLarca, as guilty and confused as she felt - if they were out of that cell, who knows what she, or Ganasan might do to Theron, or Renzo, or Anandi herself?

Renzo shrugged. "Sorry," he added. "Didn't mean to get into all that. It just strengthens my resolve to perfect the designs and get them into manufacturing."

"Your inventions in public hands, though?" Anandi asked. "HALOs are one thing, but that Disrupter Coin? If it can be deployed anywhere, it'll impact any NINE in the vicinity."

"That's true. So?"

"What if those people affected, what if they don't know they're NINE? That would be terrifying."

Renzo shrugged. "Well, better they know."

"But what if people use it to target, to visibly separate the NINE and the general public?"

"What if they did?"

That blithe statement made Anandi shut her mouth and pretend to sip her tea, though her throat closed with terror. It was one thing to read about exploits, and another to have Renzo actively agreeing to neutralize some undetermined percentage of the population.

And that wasn't the only war on the brink of eruption. Later that day, searching deeper and deeper, using Theron's Lissomes and channels, Anandi delved into the dark side of the network, following trails, making notes, and seeing more than she ever wanted to see in a lifetime.

And she found Joran Asanto. Specifically, the trail that he and his followers were leaving. There were reports of fighting in the North, in the Daro skerries, and it was crawling to the East. Bodies dropped off bridges, blood smeared across alleys and doors, forming the same strange spiral symbol, like the eye of a hurricane. Territory battles, Anandi realized. Joran's people were attacking those connected to the Savas, small-scale or seemingly untouchable.

When she told Theron of what she found, he said nothing, his eyes locked on some fixed point in the distance.

"What about a location?" was his response, finally. "Where his base of operations is?"

"Nothing consistent," Anandi admitted. "He's smart. Changes set-ups all the time. He's made powerful friends."

"Yes, my grandfather's friends," Theron said coldly. "They've changed allegiances. Disappointing."

"Is it?" she couldn't help but ask. "What do you care if they do?"

"They swore an oath."

"I haven't sworn an oath." When the words came out, she immediately regretted them. But Theron didn't react or say anything; his eyes were unfocused. What was he thinking of?

She thought back to the last time she saw Bianco Sava, the few times she'd seen him in person. He was at her birthday party in Honorwell, she remembered, at the grandfather's arm, fat and rough and balding and cruel. All this time, a secret NINE, an Osha figurehead with an ancient name.

And even with all that, still poking at Theron with a sharp stick, thumbing his nose, taking his territories, his men, his loyalties.

Will he come for you next? she wondered, eyeing Theron. *He's already killing your men. He's taunting you to come out into the light. What is with this guy, and his fixation with you?*

Everything made Anandi's head swirl. She saw Renzo with Theron, how they laughed together, how they worked shoulder to shoulder, heads bent, hands busy. And Renzo loved it. He was eager to do whatever Theron suggested.

He might as well go ahead and dye his eyes amber, join the flock.

When Theron left, Anandi felt the Lissome in her boot, pressed against her calf, hidden in the leather. To Theron's credit, she was unable to unlock it. Yet. But it was on her person at all times, even when she slept.

One more day, she told herself. *Wait for the right moment before I make any movement.*

But she was too tempted, the more access she had, the more Theron shared, the more accommodating the guards were, the deeper she drew into the secrets of Osha, the NINE, and the Savas.

It's the smart approach. It's not a betrayal. My father would not be disappointed. He knows I'm alive. He knows to keep his distance.

One more search. One day won't make a difference.

V

"You're an Insynn, I hear. Predictor of the future, through skin-to-skin contact."

Anandi stared at the pixels, at Ganasan's stoic face, body seated in a chair, with Theron sitting across from him. She'd found the cache of videos unexpectedly, swimming through the network, deeply hidden.

She paused the first video, got to her feet, checking for any sounds of someone approaching, any clicks, any surveillance. There was nothing. So Anandi eased back into her seat and resumed the video.

"When did it start?" Theron continued. "Has it changed since? Is it the only NINE skill you possess?"

No response.

Theron leaned back in his chair. "You're aware that you have an implant in the back of your head?"

Ganasan's face twitched.

That seemed to satisfy Theron, by the change of tone in his voice. "You all have one. CaLarca, too. I know where it is, I know how to extract it, and still keep you alive to see your family. I also know its purpose. Do you?"

Ganasan remained silent.

Theron tapped on the edge of the chair. "It's the Insynn trait that is puzzling me. It's a passive skill, really. It can harm through foreknowledge, and it can bring up memories, and futures, but it can't physically maim, or control, or kill. The other three skills, those are easy to hate, and fear. But Insynn, I'm stuck over.

"Precognition has its benefits, of course," Theron added. "Can help with making future plans. But is it a danger? Can it harm? That's what I'm trying to figure out. Or is it only harming the Insynn himself? Some kind of self-torture?" He laughed a little. "I understand that well enough."

Then his amber eyes fixed on Ganasan. "Of course, this is the extrasensory skill I developed."

Finally, Ganasan spoke. His voice was low, and full of disbelief. "You're an Insynn."

Theron sighed. "It seems that I am."

"But you're developing anti-NINE technology," Ganasan growled. "And holding me and my family because we're NINE. How can you justify this?"

"I don't need to justify anything," Theron said. "I'm Theron Sava."

"That name means nothing to me."

"It should," Theron said. "And it will. The name means everything. It opens doors, it opens pockets, it creates bridges. And most of the time, it provides answers. But not when it comes to you and your kind. So tell me: are you just an Insynn, or do you have more hidden talents?"

"You can't tell on your own?" Ganasan shot back.

"I've run tests, " Theron said. "I've opened up skulls. But I have so many questions. I wonder, for instance: if you have one skill, is it inevitable that you develop another, and another, and another? How can you get rid of it, altogether? Is it like a tumor, something that can be surgically removed? Is it something you have to generate within, to eradicate the bad cells? Can it be removed by cutting synapses in the brain?"

Theron leaned forward in his seat, his hands between his knees. "You're the only other Insynn I've met, so I would like to scan your brain. Test your resilience. I want to understand Insynn to its roots. If you'll permit me to do so, I'll let you rejoin your family."

"And then what?" Ganasan shot back. "We remain hostages, but as a trio?"

"You're not hostages," Theron said. "I'm not seeking a bounty, nor a reward. You're helping to make Osha a better place."

The audio cut out, and the file ended.

Dumbfounded, Anandi played it again, listening to the conversation, the threat of what was to come. Then she closed the file with a click.

She had been tracking the production of the NINE technology. Official production was scheduled to start in three days, with shipping available within the week to every corner of Osha. The last step was to make the NINE public, and create the buyer's market for such items. Theron wouldn't be asking for her help for much longer; it would be a command, and then what would she do?

She had to get through to Renzo about how wrong this all was. Public knowledge wasn't the answer. True, maybe those inventions could be used by special forces or patrol, but by the public? That would be a disaster; people against people, NINE against mortal. It could be a new kind of civil war, if it was allowed to develop.

And Anandi couldn't stay there, knowing that CaLarca and her family were imprisoned. It wasn't right, no matter her personal thoughts on the woman. She couldn't condone that, not for any cause.

She had to shut this whole operation down.

But how to do it?

Anandi leaned back in her chair, rocking in a nervous rhythm. CaLarca's cell was guarded and rigged with anti-NINE technology. Even if she distracted the guards, got the door unlocked, and disabled the technology, even if CaLarca and her family got to the front door, what then? Where would they go? What about the little boy? Would the guards shoot them if they ran?

How did Phaira do this, make these kinds of decisions? She thought back to her father, kidnapped so long ago. How easy it was to pass on the information to Phaira, knowing that the woman could handle the physical danger of saving him, and Anandi had to do nothing but wait for results. That's what she had done with the Hitodama; sat back and waited for everyone else to provide her with information and results.

With a hard exhale, Anandi let her feet hit the floor with a thump.

No more hiding. No more hiding behind screens and her father and Phaira. For once, Anandi Ajyo would step out into the light and declare her position.

Anandi had been noting patterns. Theron left the compound from late morning until early evening. The abandoned school was mostly quiet during the day, save for the faint sounds from the auditorium. There were guards, but when Theron left each day, the structure grew lax, the men so bored after such little activity. Still, they liked her. Maybe they would indulge her. And Renzo tended to work through the night, but went to his room after lunch for an hour, with that damned REM injector.

That was the time to move, that pocket.

She had to try.

* * *

When Renzo was enclosed in his quarters, Anandi made her move down the corridors, heart thumping so loud she thought her ears might explode. A Sava stood guard by CaLarca's cell, leaning against the wall, scratching at his jaw and yawning. Anandi noted the golden guns in his holster, trying to remember the Sava's first name before she spoke.

"Hi," she twinkled, trying to recall some of her old personality. "How are you? Pretty boring around here, huh?"

"You know I can't answer that honestly," the Sava said, smiling at her. "Where you headed?

Anandi jerked a thumb in the direction of the cell. "Looking to speak to the one in there. I think she might talk to me if Theron isn't around. You know? Woman to woman?"

The Sava's smile faded. "I'm not sure that's a great idea. The last time..."

"The last time, Theron interfered," Anandi reminded him.

Then she forced herself to smile. "Don't you want to get out of here? I sure do. So, if I get the intel we need, I'll make sure that you get the credit. Deal? You want Theron's favor, as do I."

The Sava hedged, eyes darting to the side.

"Five minutes. That's all I need, I promise. I've got a HALO. I'll be fine."

Was this really going to work?

"Lift your arms." The Sava's tone was sympathetic. "I have to check you for weapons."

Anandi did as told, allowing the man to pat her down. Luckily, he didn't go all the way down the back of her boot, where Theron's encrypted Lissome was stashed. Still, she made her body cowed, even shorter than it already was. It seemed to work. She was so tiny, she wasn't a threat without weapons, the Sava appeared to surmise, as he opened the door to the cell, and held up five fingers.

Anandi nodded and slipped inside.

She instantly recognized the beard and the hollow cheeks of the man in the corner. In response to her sudden entry, Ganasan scrambled to his hands and knees, one arm outstretched to protect his family. Behind him, CaLarca didn't seem to register Anandi's presence, one hand on the small of her son's back, rubbing as he slept. The drift of her fingers, back and forth, was hypnotizing.

What was Ganasan doing in there?

He must be cooperating, she realized with a sinking stomach. *Am I already too late?*

"What do you want?" Ganasan spat at her.

He hasn't seen me, she remembered. *He doesn't know who I am, or what I'm here to do.*

"I'm a friend," she told him, hands splayed to show they were empty.

Then Anandi unfastened the HALO from the back of her head, showing the trio the half-circle of silver. Her hands trembled as she lowered the HALO to the floor.

Please don't hurt me, she couldn't help but think as she stood upright. *Please don't go into my head.*

"I'm a friend," she repeated.

Then she turned from Ganasan, and peered at the walls of the cell, listening to their quiet hum. It was impressive, what Theron had come up with to neutralize their abilities, similar to the signal put out by the HALO, but cell-wide.

"If this were disabled," Anandi asked under her breath. "What could you do?"

She glanced back at the family, and she circled her finger around her head. "What could you do?" she repeated.

"We don't need your help," CaLarca's voice was cold.

"Larca," Ganasan started, but the green-haired woman shot him a look, and he fell silent.

"What are you doing here, Anandi?" CaLarca's black eyes were hard and unblinking, even as her voice remained a whisper. "Have you been watching, remotely, as always?"

That stung. She recalled the stories she'd heard about CaLarca, the bitterness, the distrust. How she called the *Arazura*, seeking Renzo, and the woman had lied to her, knowing that she'd left him, Cohen and Phaira for dead. And now Renzo was her jailer. Anandi didn't know who to trust.

But she knew what was right.

And it wasn't keeping these three in prison, no matter who they were or what they might do.

Ignoring the family, Anandi searched for the source of the current, scanning the walls and wires. Then placing her ear an inch from the current, she followed the sound of the hum.

"Don't do it," Ganasan hissed at her. "Don't touch anything. You'll get us all separated again."

"I can do this," Anandi insisted, licking a finger and tracing the edge of the current, a millimeter apart, feeling the heat. "Just let me - "

Ganasan's hand was hot around her arm.

Gasping, Anandi jerked away. Her arm was burning, as if he had branded her.

She covered it with her hand as Ganansan had collapsed with a moan.

Then the building shuddered, and Anandi stumbled.

VI.

Footsteps, and bodies clambering, and what sounded like thunder rippled through the abandoned school.

Ganasan lifted his head. "Disable this tech," he hissed at Anandi. "Disable it now!"

Then he turned to grip CaLarca by the shoulder, who stared at him with wide, frightened eyes. "You can do this. You're strong enough, I know it."

A final BOOM resonated through the building. Cracks of sunlight were suddenly visible. Voices were shouting, over the sound of gunfire.

Trembling, Anandi tried to calm her thoughts and listened, searching for the source of the current. *Shut it down*, her mind repeated, *shut it down. Flick, yank, bypass, interrupt, short out. Something!*

There, hidden behind a pipe, barely visible: a smooth mechanism the same color of the wall. Beautiful circuitry, she couldn't help but notice as she popped it open, feeling the trace of an electric shock as she dug into the mechanism, so neatly done, as she worked to bypass the securities and disable the power. The alarm sounded as soon as she started, but she could barely hear it over the sound of gunfire.

Ganasan had taken the now-squalling Bennet in his arms and stood behind CaLarca. Her feet were planted wide on the floor, fists balled, her eyes flickering between the door and Anandi.

The humming ceased, what little of it could be heard over the raucous fight outside.

In front of her, CaLarca flexed her fingers. The heat in the room started to rise.

To Anandi's shock, the shape of a knife formed in CaLarca's hand: a pearl-handled one, materializing out of nowhere.

The air in the cell shifted.

The knife was suddenly airborne, flung at the opening door.

It froze in place, shuddering, six inches from the face of Bianco Sava.

Then the knife clattered to the floor.

The sound was so much louder than Anandi expected.

CaLarca leapt at the man, a loud cry emanating from her mouth. Her cry turned into a wail of pain, as she clutched the back of her head, her body twisting to the ground.

Bianco gazed down at her with curious, cold eyes.

Then Ganasan was in front of Anandi, snatching up the knife from the floor, but he, too, was crippled with pain, his hand clasping the back of his head.

As his parents writhed, the little boy screamed on the floor. Anandi couldn't move, could barely breathe. She had disabled everything, CaLarca and Ganasan could use their NINE powers. How could they be defeated so easily?

I shouldn't have deactivated the cell, her mind screamed. *I could trigger it again, somehow. Somehow?*

There was another odd shift in the air, like a ripple of a silent wave.

And CaLarca, Ganasan and the baby tipped to the side, like toys. Anandi cried out, her hands to her mouth, as the little boy's head bounced off the floor. His eyes were closed, his mouth agape, and he was breathing, though there was a hint of blood around his nostrils. His parents breathed, too, unconscious.

In the doorway, Bianco had fallen too, but only one knee. His broad back heaved.

Then his eyes lifted and met Anandi's, gold and narrow.

She saw black spots. She was going to faint.

But she couldn't bend her knees to sink to the floor.

Her throat closed up. A thin whistling sound came from her mouth.

Pressure in her head, so great, as if she were underwater.

Then her right foot moved, and then her left.

And Anandi wanted to scream, but she physically couldn't. She couldn't control her body from sliding and slumping out of the cell, past Bianco, past the fallen guard, to where Renzo stood, hiding around the corner. Her hand shot out and snatched the Disruptor Coin from his hot grip. With the Coin coiled in her fist, Anandi hit Renzo, over and over again in the face. He tried to push her back, but she was so suddenly strong, and her blows relentless. Her knuckles split. Tears streamed down her face. When Renzo stumbled, she kicked out his prosthetic from under him, and he fell and hit his head on the floor.

Then Anandi's back hit the wall with a slam, and suddenly she could move independently again, her body shaking with relief and terror. Anandi tried to take in a deep breath but her lungs were still jerking, protesting, and she had to hold onto the wall to stay upright.

A groan, to her right, a man's voice. Renzo? No, he was still on the ground, his muddy outline she could make out through the swelling of hot tears. She turned her head to the right, thankful that she could do, and squinted.

A shadow writhed in the near-darkness. Who was that?

She heard pounding footsteps, over the roar in her ears. Bodies ran past her and leapt on the shadow. There were grunts, and curse words uttered, the smack and groan of pain.

Then the shadow drew closer, flanked on either side by the men in white. It was Theron, mouth bloodied, his face wrenched with pain, not even trying to fight back. He was shuddering. Was he having a seizure? No, his eyes were focused, not rolled back. But he was weak, and dazed.

Her brain turned in a slow crank. The Disruptor Coin had a limited range, and it affected those with NINE abilities. Theron was affected, of course he was.

Anandi's thoughts turned to ash, and her terror took over as Bianco came into view, his face a sheen of sweat, breathing heavily, but on his feet. He was holding someone's hand, someone smaller, cowed and shivering behind him, who clung with two hands to Bianco's one. The man in the middle cell, she realized with a jerk: Voss, whatever his name was. Why was Bianco holding his hand?

Bianco released Voss's hand. Renzo was awake, groaning on the ground, his prosthetic leg showing at the edge of his trousers. The HALO glimmered in the low light, looped along the back of Renzo's head. Bianco bent over, and removed Renzo's HALO roughly, taking some pieces of blond hair in the process. Then he handed it back to Voss, who took it with trembling hands.

Then Bianco turned to Anandi, and she wanted to scream; she wanted to claw through the wall instead of looking into Bianco's amber eyes.

He held out a hand, palm turned up. The Coin. She still had it clenched in her fist.

Anandi threw it at him and hid her eyes with her hands.

His heavy footsteps moved away. Anandi peered through her fingers. Bianco was striding past Theron, followed closely by Voss. Neither even looked at the man on his knees, arms wrenched painfully behind his back by the two men in white. Bianco and Voss walked to the end of the hallway, twenty feet away, and turned to face the double-door opening of the research and development center.

He locked eyes with Voss and held out his hand. Voss removed the beaded bracelet he wore, and handed it over, their fingers brushing. There was electricity in the air between the two older men; even Anandi could feel it.

Bianco unfastened the bracelet and slipped one of the black beads free.

Only then he spoke: "Bring him here."

The men dragged Theron down the hallway on his knees. Theron didn't even attempt to escape; his feet splayed behind him, his shoulders slack from effort.

Shaking so violently her teeth clacked together, Anandi crawled along the wall, following at a distance.

Bianco's arm lifted, and he tossed something underhand into the research facility.

Anandi heard a tiny *ping!* of something hard hitting the linoleum floor, and a strange, quiet whine.

Then a small *foom!*

Suddenly, Theron was thrashing against his bonds, his hair coming loose. The men in white put their knees into his back and shoved Theron back into the floor. Theron kept fighting, his shoes squeaking against the linoleum, the sound of his jacket fabric ripping.

Then Bianco had a knife in his hand and came to stand over Theron. Anandi tried to scream at him to stop, but she couldn't get a breath in.

Bianco took hold of Theron's long black hair and began to saw through it, where the red cord bound it together. Soon, great sheaths of hair were on the floor, the new ragged edges swinging around Theron's sharp cheekbone.

"Finally," Bianco said, tossing the hunk of black hair aside. "I've always hated that thing."

"Why are you doing this?" Anandi burst out. Her voice sounded so weak and scared.

"Bind her," was Bianco's only reaction. "All of them. Then bring them in to watch."

A man in white forced Anandi to her knees, wrenching her arms behind her back. She felt cold rubber cord around her wrists, tighter and tighter, and then he was dragging her down the hallway, tossing her in front of the double doors next to Theron. Bianco's men had no sympathy for Renzo; he was bound as tight as she was, and dragged to the entrance of the research facility. Then CaLarca and Ganasan were hauled from their cells, similarly bound, both still reeling from the effects of the Disruptor Coin. The baby was still unconscious, and placed between CaLarca's thighs, where she did her best to shield the boy with her body, as did Ganasan; a unit of protection, even with shuddering shoulders.

I'm sorry, Anandi tried to tell them all, with her eyes or her mind. *I'm so sorry.*

The research room burned over the next hour. The embers crawled over the floor, up the walls and tables, and melted the metal, the wires, shorted out currents, leaving behind ash, and steadily thickening smoke.

The whole time, Bianco said nothing, only nodded for Theron to be restrained, keeping watchful eyes on the others, even as tears went down soot-streaked faces, even when the baby started to wail and cough.

Voss's leg was shaking, Anandi noticed, the man's nerves seemed at their edge, whoever he was, and whatever he was to Bianco. A fellow NINE.

Theron was right, Anandi realized. *They were right to make those devices. NINE are evil. They can't help it.*

"You're dead."

Anandi turned her head at Theron's choked, furious voice.

"You're all dead." He said the last word through clenched teeth.

Voss shrank back, but Bianco crouched down in front of Theron, his knees crackling, his heavy hands on his thighs. "I thought you would have died in Kings Canyon with your parents," he said quietly. "And yet you lived."

Anandi saw the jugular vein pulsing in Theron's neck, but he didn't move from his position.

"And here you are: the survivor, once again." Bianco studied him intensely. "One by one, your cousins disappointed me. So predictable, and self-absorbed, and needy. I thought you might be different. I held out hope that after all my years of effort, it would have a worthy conclusion. A successor, a partner, even."

Anandi caught the sharp glance from Voss at that. Those words seemed to strike a blow.

Bianco rose to his feet, his joints popping again as he straightened. "I had such hopes," he continued. "I thought perhaps if you were just prodded the right way... your bodyguards being targeted had little impact. So I chose to include myself in the death tolls, thinking that might be the catalyst."

Then Bianco made a face. "I didn't think you'd run and hide behind that family. Didn't you think about how bad that looked?"

Theron spat the name: "Jetsun."

Bianco lifted a finger. "I did not authorize Jetsun's death. I accept my role of blame."

"You accept!" Theron exploded.

"I thought the enhancements would help Shantou," Bianco sighed. "Stabilize her. But NINE aren't ideal for physical experimentation, it seems. Every change made her more uncontrollable."

Bianco folded his hands in front of his belly, bowing his head as if in prayer. His voice grew quieter. "Everything has been for science, for knowledge. To understand the core of what makes us NINE. Don't think I've forgotten my goal in taking over the Savas; it's with this leadership that I can protect my children."

"Your children?" came CaLarca's snarling voice. "You mutilated Shantou. You kept her and Kuri addicted to drugs. You burned down my farm and kidnapped my family. I should - I will -"

Then her face collapsed in pain, and her forehead touched the floor beside her son, moaning.

Ganasan wriggled to get close to her "Stop it!" he begged Bianco. "Whatever you're doing, stop it!"

"That's a warning," Bianco said, lifting a finger. "Keep fighting, and I'll activate the implant to shut her down."

"What - about - Sydel?" CaLarca managed to choke out.

For the first time, an emotion crossed Bianco's face. Was it shame?

"Yes. I should have taken her." He nodded, his eyes pinched close. "Watching the development of a NINE from infancy; a prime opportunity, wasted. One of my greatest errors. I could have done so much with her."

His gaze settled on the little boy on the floor.

"And yet, another opportunity appears."

Anandi didn't know where the strength, or the courage, came from, but she was suddenly on her feet, ramming herself into the sour-smelling body of Bianco Sava. She scrambled, she kicked, she did whatever she could with her available limbs to hurt that man, to stop him from hurting anyone else.

His fist was a sledgehammer, hitting her in the chest.

A loud *crack*! echoed through the compound. Anandi's chin bounced off the floor so hard that she tasted blood and felt a loose tooth in her mouth. She curled into a ball and sucked in air, pain in her chest tightening like a vice.

"You can see," Anandi could barely hear Bianco, over the ringing in her ears, "I was careful with my own enhancements. Moderation, always, is the key, as I've learned."

A sound was rising, over the fire: sirens. Patrol was incoming. Someone had called in the attack, or the fire. Someone was coming to save them.

Then someone grabbed Anandi by the foot, and she was dragged along the floor, past Theron and Bianco, into the burning research and development space, now a horrible blend of grey ash, red fire, and orange sparks. The smoke hit her lungs hard, making her cough. The embers hit her skin, and her clothes burst into flame, and Anandi was screaming, and rolling, but everything went burning, and black.

PART FOUR

I

Daryn Ozias was a mess, the most unkempt that Phaira had ever seen. She was usually in uniform, crisp and clean, with dark brown skin and carefully pulled-back hair. Now she wore hiking clothes, and there were strands of frizzy hair at her temples. Her skin was ashy, and there were new lines across her forehead. But her eyes were still sharp, and familiar, assessing every angle of this village, and Phaira within it.

"Phaira, we need your help," Ozias announced to the valley. "I want you to join the patrol, officially as an officer of the law. Train us in how to deal with NINE, and the Sava syndicate. Help us to stop the bloodshed once and for all."

In response, Phaira turned on her heel and ran.

When the door closed behind her back, Phaira took in the deepest breath she could, and slid down so she sat on the dirt floor. Even the air seemed different when Detective Ozias showed up over the crest of the Soares Valley, with soldiers in tow; like the only sweet bit of coolness was sucked away, and there was nothing but hot, dry demands left for her to inhale.

Again, she felt the old familiar pull for mekaline. There was something about the drug that stopped the past, and the future, but kept her in the present moment, unable to process anything but the immediate sensory input, and it served as a sweet relief, again and again.

A relief that she couldn't have, ever again.

There were other options, of course. She could drink herself into oblivion. She could wander back into the wilderness. She could find the closest bridge and jump off. Phaira contemplated her options as she stared at the wall's smeared paint strokes: peach and sandstone and red brick, sponged together for texture, and abandoned nail holes with nothing to fill them.

Her grief was sudden, and vibrant: *Not yet.*

She had felt something in this valley during those one-on-one sparring matches with the other villagers, in this strange community populated with fighters of every style and weapon. She was brought to her knees, she was bruised up and down her forearms, she was cut across the brow and the stomach, new scars to add to her hundred-plus. The world was an ongoing challenge, one after another, like a rotating dance down the sand path, to another opponent, and another, and she savored every moment, even when someone half her size and twice her age managed to best her. The beauty of combat, of the body and of what it was capable of doing, it was a kind of meditation. The physical movement made everything else fade away. And then there were the smiles that followed the defeat, the outstretched hands to help her back to her feet, the claps on her back when she succeeded in felling an opponent. Phaira didn't know many names, and they never asked for hers, not the men, nor the women. But maybe that was the point of the Communia: to dissolve your labels and just exist, to push physically, to learn and absorb, to be thankful for sore muscles by the end of the day.

A religion I could actually get behind.

And yet, any semblance of happiness wasn't hers to hold. That much she had learned.

A knock at the door. "Phaira, let us in."

Phaira slid to the side, allowing the door to open.

Entering the hut, Sydel sat on the edge of the bed, eyes on the floor. When Cohen ducked under the doorframe, he caught sight of Phaira against the wall, and plopped down next to her, so close she could smell his sweat.

"How did she find us?" Phaira moaned, putting her head in her hands.

"Said she got a tip. Wouldn't say who." Then he nudged her side. "An officer, Phair." His voice was full of wonder. "Wow."

Phaira scoffed. "I can't do that."

"Why not? You'd be good at it. Probably teach them a lot."

"Cohen," she hissed. "She's trying to get me to turn on Theron. Don't you see that? It's not a real offer. She wants the information I've got to take him down."

"So what if she does?" Cohen pointed out. "If he's going crazy and hurting people, then he should be stopped."

Phaira ran her hands through her hair. "You say that like we didn't just spend the last month protecting him."

Cohen shrugged. "You really think she'd make you patrol and then take it away?"

Yes, was her mind's immediate response. *Because I am obsolete. I am wrong in every sense of the word. I am back where I belong, back in the cold, and the dirty poor, back in the obliterating sunlight, with no name, no rana, no reputation, no future.* Phaira's thoughts swirled, pushing down on her shoulders, pulling at her hands, so she had to arch her back to feel some kind of relief.

Cohen didn't seem to notice. "I think she means it, Phair. Why else come all this way? You have the advantage here. You could probably ask for whatever you want, and she'll do it."

"I just feel like we should stay out of it," Phaira muttered, rubbing the heel of her hand into her sternum. "We should stay here and keep out of it. Not until we know where Renzo is."

"I don't think Oz is leaving here without a yes."

"So what?" she shot back. "She can't force me."

Actually, she can, came that infuriating inner voice. *I could still go to jail for assaulting those patrolmen in Liera. Charges were never filed, but they could be. And what if she finds out about Kadise Sava, how I threw a knife into her chest? I didn't think anyone knew, but then Theron brought it up in the garden, when he confessed who he really was...*

His name in her head made her chest ache. She shook her head to cast it away. At least in prison she couldn't make any more bad decisions.

"I'm willing."

Phaira lifted her head, shocked.

At her reaction, Sydel lifted a hand. "I'll teach them what I know, but I don't think it will help much. Not unless any of the patrolmen are NINE in secret."

Phaira broke in. "Sydel, you don't want to - "

"I know what I want," Sydel said firmly. "I'm not hiding, and I'm not being cast as the bad guy. If people are going to know about NINE, they should see the good it can do, not just how it can harm. I need to see that it's possible when...."

There was more that she was going to say, but she closed her mouth and looked down.

"Syd's right," Cohen said, pushing himself up to a standing position. "We've been saying the same thing for months now. We shouldn't get involved. Yeah, well, we are involved, and we always have been. Maybe it's for a reason."

"This isn't some game about destiny," Phaira shot back. "Look at everything we've lost. Look what resources we have."

Cohen looked at her with a mixture of pity and disappointment. "You gotta stop running sometime, Phair."

The way Cohen said it made her insides collapse.

Is that what I'm doing? she thought. *Am I really a coward, pretending to be brave?*

"We all gotta stop running," her little brother said grimly. "Not just you. All of us. I don't know - maybe we're not meant to stay in the background."

"Maybe we're the ones who are supposed to stop all of this, once and for all," Sydel added.

What was she thinking? Phaira couldn't imagine, and for once, wished that she had cultivated more of her Eko ability so she could read minds, instead of just receiving messages.

"Nothing we do is going to make this violence stop," Phaira told them, hearing the desperate strain in her voice. "You realize that, right? We'll be on a bounty list for the rest of our lives. We'll be dragged out when we least expect it and be punished for what we've done. Or not done."

"Maybe so," Sydel said. "But I want to try. And I think you do too."

That girl knew her too well; it was unnerving.

"But you make your choice, Phaira," Sydel said, standing up. Phaira caught a hint of a sway in the girl, a wave of dizziness.

"It would be wise to hear the detective out," Sydel continued. "But whatever you decide, we'll support you."

At that, Cohen shot Sydel a look. Sydel gave an almost imperceptible shake of her head. Phaira narrowed her eyes. Those two were getting sneaky. She felt oddly lonely in that moment.

"I'll listen to what she wants," she finally told them. "But privately. Here, not out there in front of everyone."

"I'll bring her back," Sydel nodded. "Cohen, you shouldn't be here."

"I don't care if I'm in the girl section," Cohen grumbled. "This is more important than - "

"Why don't you go and speak to the patrolmen," Sydel interrupted, a patient smile on her face. "And see if you can get any other information, while their superior is not present? Any clue that the detective isn't what she seems, or has another agenda?"

Cohen's mouth opened and closed. "I can do that," he finally said, albeit gruffly.

Then he gave Sydel a smirk, and she smiled back.

Phaira watched the exchange, and couldn't place the feeling in her gut, whether it was jealousy, or shame, or deadness.

II.

Sydel soon returned with Detective Ozias in tow. The woman's gaze flicked all around the tiny hut, taking in the details, her eyebrows arched in what looked like disbelief.

Yes, I'm in a mud hut wearing strange clothes in the middle of nowhere, Phaira thought, sitting cross-legged on the ground. *Not a likely place for some miracle worker who can turn the tide of war.*

"You must be desperate, to track me down," she told the woman.

"I admit it," Ozias said. "We've lost ten patrol agents in the past forty-eight hours, and countless more are injured. And not just the patrol - pedestrians are getting caught in the crossfire."

"This is Theron, pushing all of this?" It still seemed hard to believe.

"Him, and Bianco Sava."

Phaira frowned. "Bianco Sava?" Her mind turned back to when she and Theron had gone to Bianco Sava's apartment after his death; she was suspicious of its circumstances, but the possibility of his death being true was always there. The apartment had burned, a slow burn, ignited by one of those beads on the floor, the same bead she found at CaLarca's burned-down farm in the South: some kind of strange, advanced disintegration, wiping out every trace in the slowest of burns. "He's alive?"

"He's divided the Sava syndicate, and declared himself to be the true leader. There have been breakouts of violence between the two sides, in all the capital cities. Plus, unexplainable events. People losing body and mind control."

Ozias splayed her hands open. "I wouldn't believe the stories if we hadn't met, Phaira. And I wouldn't be here if I weren't desperate to understand how to stop it. We need to understand what this NINE phenomena is, and how to defend ourselves, if we are going to quell this war."

Phaira's mind was still turning. *They have NINE on their side? How was that possible? Who would join them? Why would Theron ever want that? What is going on?*

"I meant what I said," Ozias said. "Join the force. Work with me, in the open."

Would I be Officer Byrne, or Officer Lore?

No. She was always making the wrong decision, leaping before looking, acting on impulse. She wasn't doing it again.

"Sydel is willing to teach you," Phaira finally spoke, getting to her feet. "Go make her an officer. I'm not getting involved in this fight."

The detective's voice was sharp. "How can you do that?"

"Are you going to blackmail me into service again?" Phaira shot back.

Ozias just looked at Phaira. Then, with a resigned breath, she took out her Lissome.

"I've seen the video," Phaira told the woman. "I saw Theron and CaLarca and that mess already. Anandi showed me."

Ozias winced.

Phaira's chest sank. "Why are you making that face?" she demanded.

Ozias activated her Lissome and projected an image overhead.

Phaira clapped her hand over her mouth to keep her gasp from spilling through.

A hospital bed, and a body in it. Red seeping through white gauze. Intravenous tubes in arms, feet splayed to the side. Twitching fingers. Bound arms, bound legs, and patched face, with only one side visible, and short black hair sticking up.

"What happened?" Phaira finally managed, her voice muffled through her fingers.

Ozias clicked the Lissome shut. "Confrontation yesterday. A compound got torched, and Anandi was in there. She's in critical condition. Burns to over 50% of her body. Not sure if she will pull through."

Phaira's thoughts spun so fast she thought she might vomit. Theron couldn't have done such a thing – could he? She remembered the images from the first video: his stone face, the smoke from the building, the way he looked at CaLarca. And Bianco Sava – back from the dead, and starting a war? Why? And why didn't Theron just hand over control of the syndicate? Why was he fighting back?

"Does her father know?" she asked the detective. "Emir?"

"He does." "Ozias held her gaze, so piercing that Phaira didn't dare to look away. "They're going to destroy each other, and everyone around them. And your brother Renzo seems to have gotten involved too. Did you know that?"

"Renzo - was he...?"

"No sign of him on the scene. But he was there."

A sour taste grew in Phaira's mouth. Theron had picked Renzo up, that's why he disappeared. He was with Theron. He was fighting. He was part of the reason for Anandi getting burned. Theron had turned her brother to his side.

How could she have ever thought that she loved Theron Sava?

A knock on the door. Sydel entered, a cautious glance to Phaira, and then to Ozias. "Has a decision been reached?"

Ozias extended her hand. "I'm grateful for any help you can provide."

Hesitantly, Sydel took the hand, and shook it. "I'll do my best."

Ozias let go, and reached into her back pocket, pulling out a tissue. "Here," she offered it. "Your nose is bleeding."

Sydel stiffened. Then she briskly turned her back, addressing the bleed.

A sick feeling grew in Phaira's stomach.

"We should start immediately," Ozias announced. "If that's acceptable to you. To either of you."

"In a minute," Phaira said. "A moment alone, please."

Ozias nodded, closing the door behind her. When it clicked shut, Sydel looked over her shoulder, bright red spots on the tissue pressed to her nostrils. "Phaira, it's nothing."

"That's something that looked like a mini-stroke, and two nosebleeds."

Sydel's shoulders lifted with surprise. "You saw the other bleed?" she squeaked.

"I saw the linen," Phaira told her. "You're not that good at holding secrets. What's going on?"

Sydel lowered the tissue to her side. Then, to Phaira's surprise, she smiled. "My body is turning against itself," she announced quietly.

"What - what does that mean?"

Sydel turned to face her. "You know what antibodies are, right? They're supposed to protect us from infection. But sometimes antibodies are confused and attack healthy cells. This causes... " she stumbled over the words. "Blood clots. And I've had enough that they've started to damage my organs."

"So, you take an anti-clotting medicine, or something like that," Phaira said in a rush. "Right?"

Sydel shook her head. "The clotting is dangerously fast. I'm not sure how much longer I have."

How could she say the words so nonchalantly? "Is it from using NINE?"

"I think it might be. I've felt weaker after every time I've used NINE; I just didn't pay attention before. But so many, in succession - I think one more display might kill me."

"Then why volunteer to help these people?" Phaira sputtered.

"Because it's the right thing to do."

Phaira ran her hands through her hair again and again. She couldn't get her ribs to expand. Her skin was covered with tiny pinpricks. She wanted to melt into nothingness and never be touched again. She wanted to embrace Sydel and do something, do anything to make it better. There had to be something that she could do. Some kind of treatment. They should bypass Ozias and her demands and get Sydel to a hospital. Maybe Phaira could sell the katana sword for rana. Maybe Ozias could lend them the funds; this war could wait a few days ....

"Phaira, it's done," came Sydel's voice. "I know what I want to do. I'll teach these patrolmen about NINE, and how to defend against it."

"You can't," Phaira said, feeling as though she were being strangled.

Sydel gave a pained smile. "Everyone keeps telling me that."

* * *

The training commenced. At the mouth of the valley, as a light wind drew down the scent of pine, Sydel sat on a makeshift chair before the patrolmen and patrolwomen, her cheeks pink, her head kept low, but her voice ringing through the valley, telling them all she knew about Eko, and Nadi, and Insynn. Phaira watched it from afar, arms crossed tightly, glaring at the back of heads. What would be the reaction? Would these men and women try to attack Sydel? Try to capture her? There was no telling what might happen.

Finally, Sydel stopped speaking. The silence that followed didn't last long.

"Can you demonstrate?" someone finally called out.

"I'd rather not," Sydel said. "But I can describe the sensations."

Then she raised her head to look over the crowd and catch Phaira's eye. "So can Phaira. She's an Eko."

Murmurs of disbelief went through the patrol, as heads swiveled and stared. Phaira felt her neck start to redden. "I'm not," she announced, louder than she intended. "Not really. I can't do anything."

"Phaira, please," came Sydel's quiet sigh. Phaira saw for the first time how tired the girl looked, the sickly color of her skin, how thin she had gotten. Why hadn't she noticed before?

The silence grew awkward. Everyone was waiting.

Sydel had a look of resolution on her face, that sharp-chinned look that Phaira recognized as stubbornness activated.

Internally, Phaira sighed. Then she cleared her throat, trying to keep her teeth from chattering.

"When she says Eko," Phaira started haltingly, casting looks at Ozias, who looked delighted by the turn of events. "It just means that I can receive messages. I can't project, or manipulate, or any of that other stuff."

"But you were attacked," Sydel interjected.

Sounds of interest in the crowd. A hot flush ran down Phaira's spine. Was she really going to say all this out loud? What if this was all in her head, somehow? What if she were wrong, and she told them the wrong things, and it led them all to death?

Phaira shifted her stance and wet her lips with her tongue.

"The first time," she began, "it was a memory extraction. Eko. It felt like cold fingers pushing through my head. And pressure, so much that I thought I might pass out."

She took in a breath, steadying her words. "The second time, it was a shapeshifter, Nadi, I think. And something else, too. He made me physically move, somehow."

She glanced at Ozias again. "He made me walk towards him, against my will."

Murmurs rose from the crowd. Sydel lifted a hand. "But you escaped," she called out.

"The second time, yes," Phaira said. "But barely." She touched her temple. "I have a natural defense against NINE. I don't really understand it, but it's tied into my emotions. When I allow myself to feel fear, something is generated, and I get a barrier."

Murmurs again, of confusion and interest.

"What was it like? Being on the inside with the Savas?" one of the officers asked. "You were Theron Sava's bodyguard for a time, correct? What can you tell us?"

A hundred faces turned to look at her: not just the group of patrol, but the Soares Valley residents, who had gathered at the mouth of the path to watch the events unfold.

This is the moment that Ozias wanted, she realized. *This moment, with everyone looking, asking me to reveal all that I know about someone that I swore to keep secret.*

Sydel was looking at her too. There was no Eko connection, not that she could feel, but Phaira could still hear her voice in her head.

It's the right thing to do, Phaira.

I can't. I said I wouldn't.

Sydel's voice was stronger. *Tell them.*

"Rules," she finally choked out.

Someone in the crowd repeated: "Rules?"

"There's a lot of rules," Phaira said haltingly, "and expected behavior in the Savas. They don't move far outside what they consider to be the norm."

"Like what?" one of the officers scoffed.

Phaira thought fast. "Like their weaponry. The Savas are reliant on guns. If they don't have guns, probably shockrounds would be the next level of defense. Or knives, I saw my share of those too."

"Nice to know how we can expect to get slaughtered," the same officer shot back.

"Like I said, they have patterns of behavior. The Savas rely on weapons; they aren't skilled in hand-to-hand combat," Phaira told the group, feeling more confident. "When things go outside the norm, these people get agitated. So if you negate the weapons, they will lose their footing. Then you initiate close-contact takedown. Clean knockouts."

"How are we supposed to negate the weapons?" Ozias called out.

Phaira knew how; immediately, it came to her mind how to do so. But she had to say the words out loud. She had to push past the guilt.

"Sava guns are customized to members of the syndicate. The gold ring they wear, it gives a radio-frequency-identification signal to remove the safety when in close proximity. It means only they can fire the gun. Some kind of pride thing."

Ozias spoke up, eagerness in her voice. "If we can figure out a jammer, even a temporary one, to prevent the gun from receiving the signal, we can strike. Blanket the area. Any receivers in range would pick it up and act on it, deactivating the guns."

"Yeah, but can't do that with shockrounds," one of the patrolwomen called out.

"No, but they are hard to control in close proximity," Ozias pointed out.

"There's things beyond the weapons," the same woman argued. "These NINE, whatever they are, what if they get inside our heads?"

"Knock them out before they have a chance to," Phaira said. "If they can't use their brains, I don't think they can use NINE. We exploit them for the weakness they hate to admit: they're human."

She looked to Sydel for clarification. In response, the girl lifted one bronzed shoulder.

This is all madness, Phaira thought suddenly, fighting an urge to laugh. *I'm talking like I know something. I don't know anything. This could all be wrong. It probably is wrong. And yet, here I am.*

"We?" came a cry from the back.

"You," Phaira corrected. "I'm not a part of this."

She caught the grim expression on Sydel's face, and Cohen's visible disappointment. Phaira ignored them both. They had their parts to play, and so did she, and this was what she could offer. Now to bring them back to focus.

"I'm assuming you all know the points to hit to render someone unconscious," Phaira asked the group brusquely.

No one spoke.

"For example," Phaira gestured. "On the left side of the just behind the ear and along the side of the neck lies the vagus nerve cluster, which controls the body's heart impulses. A sharp blow to this region will either incapacitate or kill the aggressor. You haven't been taught this?"

The officers shook their head. What were they teaching these men and women?

An idea struck her. "If you haven't learned how to incapacitate someone physically, this is the place to learn."

Phaira lifted her head to survey the Soares Valley residents, who continued to watch in silence, in rows, far behind. "You should all work with the residents of this valley," she announced. "If they will accept you."

As she spoke, Phaira caught the eye of the man she had sparred with before, Tomo.

She lifted one eyebrow, inquiring.

There was the slightest nod from the man. Good.

"This is a prime opportunity," Phaira said. "Learn what you can about hand-to-hand combat. Learn the hard spots, the most vulnerable spots. Understand, and master the human weaknesses of your enemy."

More murmurs of confusion, with heads swiveling.

"Do as she says," Ozias ordered the group.

The patrol men and women got to their feet. The residents came forward.

Tension billowed through the valley like a thick fog.

But soon, sooner than Phaira expected, the sound of conversations grew. And demonstrations were taking place, dust kicked up on the path in all directions; a dozen pairings on either side, grappling, learning.

Watching the activity with wonder, Phaira felt Ozias's shadow behind her. She pretended not to notice, even as the woman came to stand next to her, so close that Phaira felt the brush of Ozias's shirt sleeve on her hand.

"This is why I sought you out," Ozias said quietly. "You're a natural leader, if not a natural rule-follower."

"There's something else you should know," Phaira replied, keeping her eyes on the bouts. "Theron's built a 'work-around' into his gun. Means it can go off any time, with the signal or without."

Ozias let out a long exhale. "That information means everything. If this is the part you play in this fight, it's enough. So, thank you."

Phaira felt a hand on her shoulder.

She resisted the urge to shrug it off.

III.

The patrol stayed in the Valley for two days, working with Phaira, with Sydel, with the villagers, practicing close combat, and laying out a strategy of both attack and defense. There were tactical meetings to sort through the likely locations that Bianco Sava and his men would be found, where Theron Sava was last seen, and the communications that had been intercepted. There was going to be a confrontation somewhere in the capital city of Lea, on one of the many bridges in the city, in forty-eight hours. A peace treaty between Theron and Bianco? A joining of forces? Exchanging of money, or territory? There was no information regarding Renzo. Phaira bit her lip to hide her disappointment. Or shame. She wasn't sure what she wanted to hear about her older brother.

"We leave tonight," Ozias told her men and women. "We need all the time we can get to prepare."

There were groans of protest, quickly silenced when Ozias shot them all a look. Phaira took that moment to leave the group, and trudge back to her hut.

Sometime later, there was a knock at the door.

"Come in," Phaira said. She was standing at the window, watching the patrol gather into rows, shaking hands with the residents.

A rustle. The sweep of footprints. In her peripheral vision, Phaira saw Ozias lay something on the bed, a bundle.

A patrol uniform, Phaira realized. And a Compact firearm.

She turned to glare at Ozias. What kind of trickery was this?

"I meant what I said," the detective said. "A place with us is yours, if you want it."

"That was a trick to get me to cooperate," Phaira lashed out.

"It was," Ozias admitted. "But I've thought about it for some time now. You're smart and capable, and have a lot of admirable skills. You should be one of us."

"Special Forces didn't see me as very admirable," Phaira said sharply. "I was dishonorably discharged from the military. That disqualifies me from a position with patrol. Or did you think I didn't know about that?" She picked up the uniform bundle and shoved it into Ozias's chest.

But Ozias's eyes were glittering. "So, you have thought about it, then."

"That's what you took away from what I said?" Phaira exclaimed. "You're crazy. Get out of this valley and leave me alone."

There was a slight curl to Ozias's lip. "You're wasted here."

"These people just helped you in immeasurable ways," Phaira shot back.

"You don't belong in some monk community in the middle of nowhere." The detective's voice grew quieter. "Do you think you're such a threat that you can't be near anyone? You think I can't keep you under control? You give yourself too much credit."

Maybe I do. The thought spun in Phaira's head, breaking apart the anger.

She stared hard at the uniform. "Why are you doing this?" she challenged.

"Because I think you can make a difference."

A difference. Phaira froze with the memory. *It's what Theron said to me, back in the house on the cliffs, so long ago. Why he sought me out. Because I could make a difference. I have been clinging to that for so long, wanting his words to be true.* She eyed Ozias; did she know, somehow, about that conversation, how much it had impacted her? Could it really just be a coincidence?

"I have no veils on what you are, and what you do best," Ozias said curtly. "I need someone who's comfortable moving outside the system."

"Even if the discharge record doesn't apply," Phaira retorted, "you can't just declare me to be an officer. I'd have to complete training to be a part of patrol. Which I haven't."

"That is true," Ozias affirmed. "Handgun instruction, before one can be issued to you. Mental health training. Search and seizure procedures. Use of force, and defensive tactics. But I sense most of that would either be a waste of time, or the means to drive you back into the shadows."

Phaira didn't know what to think, nor how to move from the spot she was rooted to.

"So let's make this simple. If you take this," Ozias said, placing a hand on the folded uniform, "you need to swear an oath to protect. And I'll need a sample of your DNA. But that's all."

So I can't disappear. Ever again. They'll always be able to find me.

Phaira shook her head. "You don't want me. Trust me, you don't."

To Phaira's surprise, Ozias laughed, a husky *ha-ha*. It made her temper flare.

"I'm not getting involved," Phaira repeated. "You want to take on the Savas, you do it yourself."

The sound of laughter grew quieter, but the wry look remained on the detective's face. "What is it you want, I wonder?"

Phaira balled her hands into fists, energy coiling into her biceps, and a strange, vibrant panic in her chest.

Watching, Ozias nodded once. The tightness in her jaw gave away her disappointment.

Then she turned on her heel, and Daryn Ozias was gone.

* * *

Phaira had been searching for Sydel and Cohen for the past hour. Her blood thrummed with slow-growing anxiety, as she completed the circular path of Soares Valley. Then Phaira crossed the path into the men's side, keeping to walls and natural shadows, staying out of sight as she made her way to Cohen's red-doored hut.

The fire was out, and the beds were made. No one was inside.

But there was a note, stuck under Cohen's pillow.

When Phaira snatched it free, it fell open, revealing Sydel's light penmanship: *We have to help. We'll stay with the patrol, but we have to try and put a stop to this, once and for all. We'll be fine. No need to follow us. We will find you again.*

Phaira sank to her knees, feeling the rise of her blood pressure, how it strangled her heart, how her veins felt like they were at capacity, straining to explode.

Calm down. Calm down.

She put her fists to her temples, pressing the knuckles into the skin.

It's a gang war, came her inner voice. *Never get involved in a gang war. Ever.*

I have to follow them. Protect them.

But they don't want your protection. The voice turned ripe with malice. *What good has it done for them? Look at all the things you've let happen.*

The voice continued to berate Phaira as she stalked down the hill, back to the valley path, and kept whispering until she was back in her hut, with the door shut. Only then did she realize that the note was still balled up in her hand. She threw it across the room. It bounced off the wall, and came to rest on Sydel's bed, now stripped of its quilt and linens. Even the other residents already knew Sydel was gone. Phaira's bed was untouched. They knew she was staying. The uniform was still folded on the bed. Ozias had left the Compact firearm, too. That was reckless. Was it a mistake?

Wary, Phaira slid a hand into the folded uniform, searching for any kind of trap. Nothing but smooth, thick material. Wool blend? It reminded her of her days in the armed forces: similar feel, that smoothness. No medals this time, though, and no grey and yellow army uniform. Osha Patrol wore black, with red insignia. Trousers, collared shirt. Curious, she shook out the items of clothing, holding it up to the light. What if this was a real offer?

A different voice rose in her head, soft, but persistent: *Imagine that it is. Just imagine. No commitment. Just a dream to consider.*

A dream. Phaira didn't want to deal in dreams. She wanted to deal in facts, and logic, and anything other than her bad temper and passionate impulses.

So, logic. Phaira stared at the uniform on the bed. *I'd need to adapt,* was her first thought. *I can't move in this. What part is the most important? Probably with the insignia, and the colors. But other than that, does it matter?*

It doesn't matter, the soft voice responded. *If you want to help people. That's always been your impulse. It's a good one. Why not embrace it?*

When did Sydel become the voice of her conscience?

The rush of affection turned cold.

She's sick. And no one knows but me.

Sydel. Anandi, in the hospital, near death. Renzo, nowhere to be found. Maybe being held captive. CaLarca, and her family. There was a little boy in that video. She remembered the sound of his screaming. The look on Theron's face as he held the kicking toddler and shoved him into CaLarca's arms. The look of disappointment on Ozias's face, on all the patrol faces. They didn't fear her. They didn't hate her. They wanted her along.

They were perhaps a few hours ahead of her. She could catch up.

No. She could follow at a distance. Watch what happened. Intervene if necessary.

Maybe she wouldn't need to. Maybe she could see this peacefully resolved. Everyone in handcuffs.

Not likely.

She needed a plan. One thing at a time. She could follow, but she couldn't be seen. And not just at a distance; she needed to overhear conversations, be close enough to interject as needed. Disguised as an officer? What if Theron was there? What if he recognized her, even disguised? The thought made her both nauseous and despondent. She couldn't be seen, not by anyone. She was too recognizable, especially with her damned blue hair (why had she chosen it in the first place?). But even if it were different, her face was the same; her tattooed makeup casting permanent darkness around her eyes and her mouth, the hairline implant that projected the smooth sheen over the multiple tiny scars on her face. Again, she wondered why she'd been so impulsive to have the surgery done.

Then it hit her. The stealthsuit, the one she used in Kings. It shorted out, yes, but Renzo had taken it after. She remembered now, when they were investigating the Red, and he was dressing her wounds, he said something about applying the suit's characteristics to the *Arazura*. If he did that, he must have been able to fix and stabilize the suit. It was probably still in his cabin. If she could find the *Arazura*, she could use it, and pull other supplies...

And Renzo. He would be where the *Arazura* was, she felt sure of it. He loved that ship too much, he would never abandon it. It might lead her to Theron and where they were holing up, if Renzo was still with them.

Renzo. She had to clench her jaw to keep the rage down in her chest.

Be calm. Cool, blue focus.

A Lissome, to start. So she could figure out which direction to go, where the closest transportation was, train or bus or otherwise. Why hadn't she gotten one off Ozias, or the other officers while they were here?

Sydel had one. Would she have taken it with her? Not likely, if she was with the group.

Phaira searched Sydel's freshly-made bed, running her hands under the quilts. Nothing. She looked for any seams in the floor, the wall, even checked outside on the roof, wondering if she might have left it there. Nothing.

Her gaze turned to her own bed,: a mess, like every bed she'd ever slept in. Phaira slid her hand under one of the pillows and felt the hard edge against her palm.

The Lissome was fully charged and sprang to life when she brought it before her eyes. Instant mapping, showing her where she was on the continent. She could find the *Arazura*, easily, as long as Renzo hadn't changed the connection code. But what about Cohen?

Solar trackers. The sudden idea made her gasp outloud. The solar tracker. Renzo and Cohen still wore the same boots; the trackers would still be in the hidden back seam of the leather. It was a vow they had made, years ago, when Phaira secretly joined the armed forces. The trackers were archaic, and embarrassingly engraved, but Renzo insisted that she keep one on her person at all times. Then Cohen got between the two, as he always did, and said he would wear one too, to appease them both, if they would just please stop yelling at each other. It was the solar tracker that helped the brothers find Phaira in Midland, in Jala Communia; it was how Renzo found Kings Canyon and rescued them all.

She didn't have hers anymore; it was in that rock pile from the collapse of the Kings Canyon base.

But Cohen might. She had to hope that he would remember and activate it. Maybe he had already.

She punched in the code to the trackers they shared, waiting as a connection was attempted.

It came up negative.

Not yet, then. She made a silent plea to Cohen to remember. If only she'd thought of it sooner and could have told him.

She had to trust him to think of it himself. Take care of himself, and of Sydel.

First, the *Arazura*.

When Phaira took her leave of Soares Valley, every resident gathered to watch her go. It was strangely comforting. Tomo was at the forefront, bidding her farewell. He had provided her with a change of clothing and a satchel to keep them in, plus provisions and water for the hike, and some spare rana, which she took with some embarrassment.

"Thank you," she told him. "For everything."

"You're one of us," Tomo replied, his expression neutral. "You always have a place here."

Phaira didn't know what to say to that. But she did look back once.

Then the mist hit, the planes changed, the Valley was out of sight, and she was alone.

The air was brisk, chilling her lungs to the edge, but her legs were still strong, churning through the rocks, heading east. Theron's katana was strapped across her back, tight and sheathed. The world was silent save for the sound of her footsteps through the brush. Phaira remembered how she felt the last time she was walking through these plains, only days ago; buried under shame and barely able to function, feeling only the trace presence of her brothers, of Sydel, on either side of her, and wanting nothing more than to find a precipice to throw herself over.

Now it was different. Phaira still felt that little dark thread that wove through her, thickened with emotion. But layered on that was a different kind of shame: developing feelings for someone like Theron Sava, letting herself get so distracted and foolish, forgetting what was important.

What do I want?

Phaira brought up her Lissome, and the blinking target that indicated the current location of the *Arazura*. A rush of relief went through her every time she could pinpoint it. The connection code hadn't been deactivated yet; she still had a path to follow.

As the day passed, and the sun slid overhead, Phaira stopped a few times to rest, to eat, to hydrate. In the open air, the voices in her head had quieted somewhat, still there, but the volume had been turned down. She saw no other travelers on the way, only horizons and the edge of the Cyan Mountains. Would she have to sleep outside? It was very possible, unless she wanted to keep travelling in the dark. She thought of Renzo, how they had reluctantly embraced each other for warmth. What was she going to say to him? What was she going to do when she found him?

What do I want?

As Phaira hiked, her brain replayed scenes from her life like a continuous film reel. She thought about her father, and her mother; both dead, both frayed and grey in her memories. Little moments when she was younger, with Renzo, with Cohen. How Cohen used to cling to her. How she felt some sense of motherly affection towards him, the kind that she would never replicate in life. She had been so consumed with being invisible, had she bothered to notice anyone else in the world?

The day wore on. Phaira felt the strain of her muscles, her arms, her back, her thighs. Her always-reliable strength, coming to her aid again and again. She wondered how long it would last, when she would start to feel an ache in her hips, or her knees might give out. Young to think about such things, perhaps, but she'd been so physical for so long, it occurred to her as she moved up a rocky incline that she was probably in for some significant pain. If she managed to grow old.

What do I need?

The question echoed again and again, as Phaira hiked into a village. She found rides with people passing through, then she hitched on the back of a passing train. Resting when she found a pocket of safe space. Eating when she couldn't stand it any longer. Handing over rana to eager hands only when necessary, and when she made it clear that the funds secured silence. Crawling east, one kilometer at a time, and her thoughts on constant rotation, a computer processing and spitting out potential answers.

Many times, Phaira's thoughts turned to Nox. She remembered him vividly, his patrol uniform, that silly red beard he grew in the last year.

If I had followed him out of the military, and into public service, I could have pursued Nican Macatia when he attacked Renzo. Built a case against him, instead of throwing him off a bridge, and ruining all my family's lives.

If I could go back, I would. I would take the desk job, and complain about the lack of action, if it meant....

Meant what?

Those thoughts ground to a halt, despite her desire to believe that any part of them were true. Because they weren't. She would have been like Nican Macatia: seeking out thrills, making dumb choices, her ego overwhelming any sense of humanity. It didn't matter if Phaira were behind a desk, or in the field. Trouble would always find her. It always had.

And in a secret, small way, she loved that it did.

I need to know I'm worth something.

I need to be seen.

One hundred kilometers from West Lea, and the *Arazura's* location, Phaira negotiated a ride with a passing trucker, who let her climb into the cargo bed already full of crates. In there, Phaira stared up at the night sky, feeling the rumble of the road through her thighs. She activated her Lissome, and then the LRP network, and searched for her name. That listing was still there; posted by someone anonymously, so many weeks ago, with a blurred picture of her face, a list of her physical skills and suspected missions, and that name she spat out in a moment of pressure that now followed her everywhere. *Phaira Lore.* Like some superhero name. It still made her cringe to hear it.

Her gaze lifted to the network description: *LRP: Locate - Retrieve - Protect.*

Maybe it was time to embrace what people saw her as.

Phaira clicked the Lissome shut. Cohen and Sydel were right. No more hiding. No drugs, no sex, not any other distraction. If she wanted to be seen, and be worth something, she had to become someone worthy. Not just search for it from outside sources, but something inside that made her feel worth a damn.

I've made so many mistakes as Phaira Byrne.
I won't as Phaira Lore.

* * *

The *Arazura* was unlocked, and silent as Phaira crept through. When she peered through the doorway of Renzo's cabin on the *Arazura*, her heart jumped.

Renzo's pallor was sickly, his cheeks were thick with stubble, and he wasn't even wearing his prosthetic; it was propped up in the corner.

When Renzo saw her, his jaw dropped. Then his eyes darkened, and his chin jutted out.

"I made a mistake," he spat.

"Yes, you did," Phaira shot back. She could tell by the way his jaw was working that he wanted to accuse her of making so many mistakes herself. Let him try. It didn't negate what he'd done.

"So, are you a Sava now?" she flung out, like a knife.

"No." Renzo's voice was strangely distant. "I never was."

He lifted his gaze to hers. "I made a mistake," he repeated with a growl.

"So fix it," Phaira said. "Get up and fix it."

"I'm not doing anything," Renzo snapped. "You had the right idea all along. Just don't care about anything. Stay detached, take what you can get to survive, don't engage, don't care...."

Phaira stared at him. *Is that what he really thinks of me?*

"Did you get hurt in the fire?" Phaira finally asked, trying to dampen down her hurt. She searched him for any bandages, a hint of smell in the air. The ship was musty, but nothing that spoke to infection or burnt skin.

"I lost everything." The flat way he said the sentence, she didn't know what to think.

"So that's what you're doing in here?" she accused. "Hiding?"

"I'm not hiding," Renzo said hotly.

"Oh really? Have you gone to see Anandi in the hospital?"

Renzo's face drained of color. "You - you know about that?"

Phaira wanted to grab him and shake him until his teeth clacked. "Get up," she demanded. "Get out of bed and stop feeling sorry for yourself."

Renzo glared at her with the intensity of the sun and didn't move.

Phaira felt heat rising in her palms. She would grab him. She would fight him. She saw all the moves to come in her mind, like a flicker of cards.

She balled her fists instead. "And Theron?" she tried. "Is he hiding out, too?"

Renzo's eyes shifted. "I don't know what he's doing."

"When did you see him last?"

"When the fire broke out."

Phaira waited for more details, but Renzo remained silent. Who was this brother of hers? What kind of person had he become, when she wasn't looking?

"I need the stealthsuit from Kings," she finally told him, keeping her voice low and steady. "And reinforcements."

Renzo's face twisted. "Why? What are you getting into now?"

Me? she wanted to splash back in his face like boiling water. Instead, she told him: "I know about the bridge confrontation. Cohen and Sydel left the valley before me. They want to try and stop the fighting."

To Phaira's surprise, a gasp escaped Renzo's mouth. Then he buried his face in his hands.

"Why? Why would they do something so stupid?" she heard him mutter through his fingers.

"Why have anyone of us done the things we have?"

Renzo said nothing, but Phaira saw how tight he clenched his jaw under his hands. Weariness suddenly fell over her, like a heavy blanket; she even felt her knees buckle with the fatigue.

"Ren," she began quietly. "I'm following."

Renzo still didn't move or look up from his hands.

"At least, I'm going to try to. I'm hoping Cohen will activate his solar tracker," she continued. "He hasn't yet, so I don't know his position right now."

"I forgot about those," Renzo said through his fingers. He glanced at the floor, where his boot lay, empty of the prosthetic. "Is that how you found me?"

"I tracked the connection code to the *Arazura*, dummy. You never changed it."

"You're right. That was dumb of me."

Phaira studied her older brother; how there were new lines on his already-wrinkled forehead, how loose his clothes were. How broken he seemed.

"I don't even know if Cohen will show tonight," she blurted out. "Or Theron, or any of them. It could be a trick."

The way Renzo took in a sharp breath, like he was getting a knife in the gut, gave her the answer. She couldn't read her older brother's face, or thoughts.

This was bad. The severing was bad this time.

"Ren, I have to go," she finally said. "It's almost midnight."

She turned to leave, but hesitated, her hand on the door-frame, running down the cool metal. Familiar.

Then she looked over her shoulder at her brother. "Will you watch remotely? From here?"

Renzo glanced up at her.

Phaira tried to give him a smile, but her mouth wouldn't work. "You can find some cameras to hack into by the bridge, I'm sure."

Renzo frowned. "What are you asking me, really?"

Scenarios flashed through her head. Death. Chaos. All likely. She needed a tether.

"If I call you for help, will you come?"

Renzo pressed his mouth together.

"Will you come if I call?" Phaira asked again, emphasizing each word.

Renzo got up from the bed, balancing on one foot. Holding on the edge of the wall, he hopped to a crate in the corner, buried under clothes and tools that clanged against the ground as he shoved them aside. He rustled through the contents and pulled something free. White and rippling. Familiar.

"Did you stabilize it?" she asked, stung by his silence. She was on her own, she knew that now.

Renzo tossed it to her. Then he inched his way back to the bed and flopped on his back with a grunt.

Finally, Renzo spoke: "You were sleeping with Theron this whole time?"

In this moment, she hated her brother and everything he represented; every way in which he brought out her worst parts.

In her silence, Renzo snorted, in a way that made her temper flare.

Words pushed at the inside of her mouth: insults, accusations.

A new path. A new direction, she reminded herself. *Away from drugs, and pettiness, and letting emotions get the better of me.*

He is who he is. And so am I.

She turned away from her brother, balling the stealthsuit under one arm.

But Phaira paused mid-step, looking over her shoulder. "I care more than you think," she announced. A final fling of a knife.

Then Phaira exited the cabin, heading to the *Arazura's* lower level.

V

When the twin moons were overhead, and the purple
night was starless, Phaira stood before the East-West
Lea bridge. Construction warnings had removed all traffic from
the bridge; false signs to ensure that this tenuous, momentous
meeting was not interrupted.

The wind cut through the stealthsuit as Phaira walked with
the lightest stride, no sound against the ground as she checked
for signs of surveillance. Not that she could be seen on video, if
there was. Her assumptions had been correct; Renzo had stabi-
lized the old white stealthsuit, and it sprang to life the moment
she activated it, to her pleasure. Now it remained humming,
and her invisibility was constant, as she wove through down-
town Lea, and made her way past the construction warnings
onto the bridge, past the support frames, heavily bolted, tri-
angles in every configuration. There were so many different
nooks that she could duck into, but she was hesitant; she didn't
want her legs to grow numb, and inactive from waiting.

It was strange to be on the asphalt, so high above the river.
The river drowned the sounds of the city out, the further she
walked along. She'd never been on this particular bridge, but
she had stared at one like it, in one of many North industrial
cities she'd lived in, wondering what it would be like to throw
herself off. If it would hurt. If it wouldn't work, and she'd be left
broken forever.

To ground herself, Phaira felt the weapons on her frame: the katana down the length of her spine, the knife at her hip, and the Compact firearm that Ozias had given her, all strapped down, so she could move, but easily accessible, in case she couldn't. And she wore a HALO, dug out from the *Arazura*; still active, she hoped, as she looped it around the back of her head.

Midnight was approaching. Phaira paced along the center of the bridge, walking heel to toe to avoid any sound. The wind grew louder, making strange sounds through the metal beams.

Then, movement.

Barely perceptible, but Phaira caught it, and froze in mid-step, instinctively checking to make sure the suit was still activated. She was still invisible.

But shadows were moving on both ends of the bridge.

On one side, a familiar silhouette, next to a smaller, thinner one. Phaira held her breath. Cohen and Sydel. They were walking out into the bridge, holding hands. No one followed them. Phaira craned her neck, searching for signs of Ozias, or any of the patrol. They had to be out there somewhere, waiting and watching. Wouldn't they?

Just because they said they went with patrol doesn't mean they were telling the truth.

Panic strangled her throat, and she tilted her head back to stretch it out, to breathe and compose herself. She had just assumed that patrol would be there. What if they weren't? What if Cohen and Sydel had stolen away on their own, and Ozias had no idea?

She had to get a signal out to the detective, somehow. Phaira pressed her lips together, feeling the sweat at her brow and in the small of her back. Maybe she could activate her Lissome, steal a quick message, and no one would see. But it would mean pulling the device out, and activating it, and sending out a signal that could be tracked, could pinpoint her location on the bridge.

Did she dare, when she was already in the perfect place to observe, and react?

The back of her neck prickled. Without turning her head, Phaira slid her gaze to the opposite side of the bridge.

Pale silhouettes walking in sync, men, and women, wearing white, surprisingly, white so blinding that they radiated. Their dark shadows crept behind them, stretching across the length of the bridge, like bodyguards to be flung as needed.

The one in the front, she knew that man. She flashed back to Anandi's party, so many weeks ago in Honorwell, when chaos erupted, and Theron's grandfather was there, making threats. The man lumbering down the bridge had been there, whispering into the grandfather's ear.

Bianco Sava.

Staring at his approach, Phaira took little sips of air, and consciously flexed each of her calf muscles, then leg muscles, then shoulders, biceps and forearms in a steady pattern. In her peripheral vision, she saw that Cohen and Sydel were in the center of the bridge, ten feet. Could they sense her? Could Sydel, even with Phaira wearing the HALO? She watched for any sense that her brother and her friend could tell that she was crouched, invisible, and watching.

As Bianco drew closer, Cohen put his hand on the small of Sydel's back, as if to steady her. Did he notice how ashen she was? Phaira longed to reveal herself, to turn off the HALO and reach out to Sydel, but she grit her teeth and remained still.

Neither turned their heads in her direction, but both watched as Bianco and his followers drew closer. Ten in all, behind him. Phaira didn't recognize any of the faces, but she could smell them: the cologne, the sweat, the low-level anxiety, along with the stink of the river below. Briefly, she wondered whether she emitted any kind of odor, or if Bianco was watching with heat-signature. Suddenly, her plan to be invisible on the bridge seemed incredibly silly.

Bianco took the lead then.

He looks ridiculous in white, Phaira thought. In the color, he was pale and sour, and smug, his stomach stretching the lapels of his jacket.

Sydel tensed, gripping Cohen's hand tighter the closer Bianco came.

He stopped six feet from her, his arms behind his back, looking her up and down.

"My daughter," was his only remark. "Hmph."

"I'm nothing of yours," Sydel said, her voice higher-pitched, but with a bite in her words.

"All right, no-daughter-of-mine," Bianco said smoothly. "Why are you here? You were not invited."

Sydel lifted her chin. "I'm here to tell you to stop."

Bianco barked out a laugh. "Stop what? You'll have to be more specific."

Sydel spoke through her teeth, her voice half-carried away by the wind. "You might think that you're untouchable, but you're not."

Bianco's men oohed and laughed, but their leader held up a hand. Phaira's eyes went to the sleeve of his jacket, the stiffness of his right arm. There was something about it that set off suspicion. Artificial? A weapon concealed?

"Are you challenging your father to a fight?" Bianco asked, much quieter, and with far more interest.

Phaira's stomach rolled. What did that mean?

Cohen glanced at Sydel. Bianco caught it too. "Your boyfriend isn't fond of that idea."

"I make my own decisions," Sydel said.

Bianco cocked his head, peering at Sydel with such intensity that it made Phaira squirm. There was sweat on her upper lip, and she longed to wipe it away. Cohen's hand tightened at the small of Sydel's back.

"I hear you're sick," Bianco announced. "Perhaps even dying?"

Sydel gasped. Cohen jolted hard. Phaira felt the rip in his heart as if it were her own. *Cohen,* she lamented. *I'm sorry.*

Observing their reactions, Bianco sighed. "So it's true? What a waste."

Phaira's temper flared at that, and she had to push her fingernails into her palms to calm her anger. Cohen wasn't holding it back much better; Phaira could feel the tension rippling off Cohen, how he clenched his jaw under his beard. She heard the men behind Bianco, chortling. They enjoyed the tension, it seemed. Phaira found the jugular vein in each of their necks, marking them with an invisible X.

Sydel was the first to speak, throwing out her first accusation: "Did you hold CaLarca, in the time between the Kings

Canyon massacre, and when we found her at the bottom of that crevice? Those two weeks?"

Bianco didn't blink. "I did."

"Why?" Cohen burst out, surprising them all.

"Curiosity," Bianco said. "First, to see what she was capable of. Then to ensure that she could be controlled as needed, so she could remain close to you and determine your potential."

Phaira shuddered at the terminology. And Sydel was equally disgusted, given the look on her face. "You've been controlling her? From afar?"

"Keeping watch," Bianco corrected. "Ensuring she does what I want. Reacts as I wish, and tests your limits, Sydel."

Phaira's brow furrowed. So, the CaLarca on the ship, that wasn't the real CaLarca? She had been unconsciously prodded to behave a certain way? Somehow, Phaira had a hard time believing that the sour, combative woman was any other way.

"If you have been with the Savas all this time," Sydel began slowly. "You knew about Kings Canyon, and Keller Sava. You knew they were hunting the rest of the NINE down, and they were working with Huma and other NINE. You must have known. "

"Of course I knew," Bianco corrected. "I gave Keller Sava the inspiration. Told him about Huma. I was curious to see what he would do with it, and all the information I left in the underground base. It went further than I thought it would, though they were all a disappointment in the end."

Sydel took a step forward. Phaira watched Cohen's hand move to take hold of Sydel's elbow. She saw how his throat rippled with a swallow. But there was more: there was tension through his right side, to a focal point on his thigh. He was armed, Phaira realized. He was activating something. She swiveled her head, searching for any signs in the darkness, on the river bank, in the windows, so far away on the skyline.

"That's enough talk, no-daughter," Binaco said finally. "I have an appointment to keep, and I would suggest you get off this bridge. One stay of execution is all I can offer."

"This is my business," Sydel said. "You, and Theron Sava, all the destruction you are causing and the people you've hurt. It stops tonight."

More laughter from the group behind Bianco, but there were some wary expressions as well, and hands sliding under jackets.

"What are you going to do, Sydel?" Bianco murmured, so quietly that Phaira had to strain to hear. "Do you have the courage to reach inside my brain and kill me?"

She could do that? Phaira stared at the girl's profile, both aghast and curious. What a power to have, if that were true. And why wouldn't it be? After everything that Phaira had seen, anything was possible when it came to Sydel. If she were to do such a thing as reach into someone's brain and shut off life, what would it be like? A snap, a fall, like a row of dominos?

Her interest turned to dread. Sydel's health was on the brink. If she tried to use her NINE abilities in any way, she might die. Bianco didn't know that, but Phaira did. Would she dare?

"Do you think you can do it before I can?" Bianco continued to whisper. "Are you certain of that?"

Don't, Sydel, Phaira begged in her mind. *It's not who you are, even if he's horrible and deserves it. Let me do it.* She felt the fire in her hands, the muscles and the tense joints, and saw all the places she could strike at that fat, old man. Her focus was cooling and narrowing, blue swimming through her body. The element of surprise, the exposure of arteries, the folds of his neck, begging to be cut. Her head lowered, and adrenaline pulsed through her limbs.

Now.

Phaira reached back to remove the blade from her back.

Her hand stopped when she heard a whine.

It came from somewhere behind Bianco; he seemed annoyed as he turned to speak over his shoulder. Phaira lowered her hand, confused, hoping the swish of her movement had been masked by the wind and river.

A cowed older man appeared, dressed all in brown, holding a toddler boy in his arms. The man had heavy lines in his face, and held the boy tightly. The boy had dark brown hair, and golden skin, and his face had the chubbiness of infancy. He was the source of the whine, rubbing his eyes and clutching a stuffed rabbit. When his eyes opened fully to look around the bridge, Phaira could see that they were wide and black.

Phaira's insides froze. The video of the assault, of Theron and CaLarca. The boy in the video, passed over to CaLarca. Covered in blood and dirt. CaLarca's son.

This was CaLarca's son.

Phaira wasn't the only one who made the connection. Sydel's jaw had dropped at the sight. Cohen's brow furrowed, looking from Sydel to Bianco. Then realization came over him. "That's CaLarca's kid. Why do you have CaLarca's kid?"

Bianco reached out for the boy, who shrank away from the man's meaty hands. Bianco pointed his finger into the boy's face, staring the child down until he cowered and allowed himself to be taken. The older man let him, keeping his eyes on the ground.

"I made a mistake, Sydel," Bianco announced, hoisting the boy against his shoulder. "I should have raised you myself. Taught you to develop your skills properly, instead of wasting your life in some country commune."

This time, Cohen did reach out and hold Sydel back.

"Instead, I placed my care and attention into unworthy children," Bianco said, gazing into the boy's frightened face, "who grow up to be disappointing men."

He's talking about Theron, Phaira realized with a start.

"Now a new chapter begins," Bianco continued, holding the boy tighter. "A chance to get the experiment right this time, from the start."

"No." Sydel's voice carried across the bridge. "No, you won't. I won't let you."

"Unless you'd like to come with me, and ensure the boy's safe upbringing," Bianco said smoothly. "Show him everything you wish you'd learned."

Phaira saw the temptation cross Sydel's face; the notion to self-sacrifice, to help someone in the little time she had left. Presenting a good role model of a NINE, like she had always wanted.

Bianco caressed the boy's face with his hand. When he did, the boy dropped his stuffed rabbit.

The man in brown stooped down, as Bianco continued to speak: "So, Sydel, I - "

A flash of metal.

A pearl-handled knife swung in and out of Bianco's side.

Five rapid strikes, making loud puncture noises.

Hitting major organs, Phaira knew immediately, as she held back her scream of surprise.

The man in brown snatched the boy from Bianco's surprised hands. His clothes were now sprayed with blood, but his head was different: not dark-haired and male, but braided and female.

CaLarca.

And before Phaira could react, CaLarca and her son vanished, as if someone had pulled a shade down over them. There was no trace, or movement, or breath of either of them, despite the frantic henchmen and their panicked yells to grab her and find her. Phaira craned her neck, searching. How could she just disappear like that? How did she turn into that man?

In the center of the bridge, Bianco stood, trying to hold in his insides.

Human, Phaira thought with a sneer. *Mind control all you want, but you bleed like everyone else.*

Ten feet away, Sydel held onto Cohen, tears on her bird-thin face.

"Daughter," Bianco rasped, reaching out a bloodied palm. "Heal me."

Sydel stared at her father, her fist pressed against her breast-bone as if to hold in her heart.

Syd, don't! Phaira pleaded with her mind, tempted to rip off her HALO and try to project.

"Heal me," Bianco repeated, desperation in his voice.

Slowly, Sydel shook her head back and forth.

Bianco fell to his knees.

Behind him, ten gold pistols were drawn in unison, glinting in the moonlight, directed at Cohen and Sydel.

Phaira sprinted forward and leapt on Bianco's back. The man squawked with surprise, flailing at the sudden pressure. The Savas lowered their guns, dumbfounded at what was going on, until Phaira deactivated the suit, pressing the barrel of her Compact firearm into his temple.

"He's going to die now, or in ten minutes," she announced to the group. "If you lower your weapons, you have time to get him the medical attention he needs."

She was buying only seconds with her demonstration, she knew that. It was ten against one. They would shoot her dead before she had a chance to fire.

But it was a final thing she could offer to her family: a head start.

But Cohen and Sydel weren't running. Their eyes were bugged out, and sweat shone on their faces. Their bodies stiff. Unmoving. Frozen.

"You stupid woman," she heard Bianco rasp.

His hand was around her ankle, squeezing. Crushing.

Phaira gasped, feeling the muscles bruise and bleed, the bone on the brink of breaking. Cybernectics.

With all her strength, she bashed the hilt of the Compact into the Vagus nerves on the side of his neck. Bianco gave a surprised groan, and his body buckled to the asphalt.

Over the roar of the river, Phaira heard a heavy exhale from Cohen, and a higher-pitched one from Sydel; the control had been lifted. They were stumbling, trying to break into a run.

Tiny clicks, and ten gold barrels lifting.

More time. Give them more time.

Pushing through the searing pain in her leg, Phaira leapt at the group of Savas, drawing her katana and slicing at any gold and white she could see through her blurred vision. Amid the cries, Phaira held her breath as she swirled, waiting for pain to rip through her.

But there were just clicks in the air.

And soon, panicked gasps.

The signal was jammed. The Sava weapons were offline. Patrol was here.

Gold guns clattered to the bridge, useless. And Phaira cut through the open hands and panicked screams that followed. Spatter here, spatter there, on the white stealthsuit, different patterns, depending on the artery.

A shot rang out.

Phaira flinched. Breach in the signal? It wasn't possible; no, it wasn't possible.

Distracted, she took a punch to the jaw by a Sava and stumbled. Someone took a swipe with a knife, cutting her across the thigh. More fists, more blows, and she was surrounded, and pummeled, and she couldn't move...

"Phair!" she heard Cohen's cry.

He was coming back for her.

"No!" she gasped out, her palm extended, as if to push him away, before her arm was grabbed, and she was flipped over, hitting the asphalt hard. Someone stomped on her ribs for good measure, and she gasped for breath, rolling on her side.

Through the legs of the Sava men and women, she saw the glint of metal, not gold, but silver and tiny, something that could fit in a boot.

Bianco, lying in a pool of spreading blood, his arm extended. Aiming.

Another shot rang out.

Ten feet away, Cohen's body jerked.

She heard the tear in his skin.

She heard the swallow of his surprise as he fell.

And he was bleeding; there was so much blood pooling in his clavicle, even as Phaira pushed through the group of Savas and put her hands against his pulsing neck, howling at Cohen to stay awake. Not him, not him, this wasn't happening. Her baby, her baby brother. She couldn't breathe, she couldn't feel her heart, or her extremities. White, searing pain, that was all she could register, so violent that it yanked at her breastbone, threatened to split her ribs. Her stomach was straining to come out of her throat, and every sense was too much: too much copper smell, too much wet.

It took forever, and no time at all, before Cohen's mouth went slack, and his eyes dilated, and Phaira could feel the warmth draining out of him. She screamed at him to wake up. She begged to be blasted by a similar shot and black out from the agony; to turn back time and take the shot for him, like she was supposed to do, like she was always ready to do.

The surviving Savas had gotten ahold of Sydel. She was clawing at them, screaming, trying to pull their hands off her arms and body. Her body was shaking. Her eyes were rolling in her head, and her hair was standing in tufts. Something was building. Familiar, through the dark water of Phaira's perception.

Then the world exploded in blinding white. Roaring sounds came in waves, again and again. Phaira was torn from Cohen's body, rolling along the ground. Her head was screaming, her skin was burning, and it wouldn't stop. She tucked herself into a ball, her arms over her head, kneeling on the katana blade to hold it down, her screams of pain inaudible to her own ears.

Just as quickly as it came on, the light was gone.

Waves of heat passed over Phaira. She smelled burnt hair, and skin. Her own?

She struggled to open her eyes. The stealthsuit had been partially burned off her, hanging in strips, some still smoldering. She ripped it off, checking for the HALO at the back of her head. Still on.

Ahead of her, corpses in white suits lay on the ground in a radial pattern, limbs splayed. Sydel was in the middle of the circle, face-down, motionless. The blood around Cohen's body bubbled. Bianco had been flung into his back, his exposed intestines showing sear marks, as his belly heaved. The other bodies she'd cut down were also giving off steam.

Everyone was burned. Everyone was dead.

Footsteps. Someone was coming. Ozias? The patrol? Where were they?

Through her wavering vision, she could make out a dark silhouette, followed by a line of others, picking through the sea of bodies.

Stop, she tried to say. *Get away from here.* But her voice wouldn't work. She coughed, trying to get the burning sensation out of her lungs, blinking furiously to clear her eyes. Finally, her vision sharpened.

Theron Sava stood over Bianco's shuddering body, his Compact firearm pointed at the man's forehead. His long hair was gone, shaved to the skull, his features stark and sharp, dark circles under his eyes. What had happened?

Before Phaira could react, Theron pulled the trigger.

The *BANG* echoed across the bridge.

Phaira stared, taking in shuddering breaths. For some reason, she thought killing a NINE would be tougher. But he was blood and brain and bone, what was left of Bianco Sava. He was dead. It was done.

Now Theron was walking. He wasn't looking at her, or anyone on the ground. His followers (how many were there?) all in black, silently trailing their leader, picking through the dead bodies. Phaira struggled to push herself to a seat, wincing and hissing through her teeth at the raw burns on her arms.

Theron's boots stopped beside Sydel's limp arm. Phaira heard the click of the safety being removed. Only then did he lift his gaze and look directly at Phaira.

"It has to be done," he announced. "You know it does."

"No," Phaira rasped.

"If not by me, someone else. Look what she's done. Look what all these NINE have done."

Phaira pushed herself to her knees, coughing the words. "She didn't – you can't just - don't do this."

"No." There was a strange flatness in his voice. "If I don't, it'll never stop. No one will ever stop. Everything deserves to burn to the ground. Everything and everyone."

Phaira saw the bones in his wrist move to the skin's surface, the bend of his index finger.

No, her mind screamed, as she reached out a hand, already knowing that it made no difference. She could smell the gunpowder, about to explode.

Theron grimaced, and looked down at his Compact. He wasn't pulling the trigger, she realized. His hand was shaking, but the index finger wasn't bending. He banged his palm against the side of it. Jammed?

A moment. A chance.

Phaira leapt, and Theron had to lean back to avoid her right hook. His followers went to grab her, but she barely noticed the motion, because she needed to hit something; she needed to crush her fist against someone's face; she needed to exert all this horrible, horrible energy inside of her, and he was the one who started it all. He was the villain from the start, worming between them all: inventing with Renzo, watching over Cohen, sleeping with Phaira. She swung, again and again, and he managed to avoid the blows, but barely, stepping back, sweeping his wrists to block, hearing the smack of her fist in his palm as he threw her arm away, pushed her foot away.

"Is this what you wanted?" she yelled at him through her choking tears. "Is it?"

That last statement was the last time Phaira could recall having any semblance of thought. After that, everything was white and red and black, and her extremities seemed to move independently, and there was blood, and bruising, and his familiar smell. He was fast, but she was faster, and she knew his fighting style now, how he used her energy against her, so she let her instincts take over, and everything was glorious; the pressure on her elbow, the heel of her palm, the toe of her boot, as they made contact, as the sound of crunching hit her ears, his exhale of surprise, and later pain. He got in some hits, too, but she barely felt the crunch of her joints. He was sweating now, and he was growing more vicious. But things were blue, and frozen, and focused, and her only intent was to cripple him, to pinpoint every joint, every soft spot, all the places that she knew he was vulnerable.

Backing away from a strike, her foot struck something. Her katana, lost when the blast hit. No, his katana, glinting under the bridge lights.

Memories flashed, and it made her rage burn even hotter.

Phaira dropped to her knees, spun to avoid a kick, and snatched up the blade. Then Phaira leapt back to her feet and lashed out with a series of strikes. Theron tried to block with his arms, but his shirt was being cut, one swipe at a time.

With one last burst of strength, she slashed it across Theron's chest.

Drops of blood spattered the asphalt.

Phaira clutched her ribs, heaving, the blade dragging on the ground.

Blood was everywhere. There was so much of it.

Theron was stumbling backwards.

Theron was going over the bridge rail.

The river crashed underneath the bridge, churning and black. Theron hung by his left hand, his tattered shirtsleeve exposing his arm. Phaira grabbed his wrist, but both were slick with sweat and blood, and he kept slipping from her grasp.

"No, you're not," Phaira gasped, straining every muscle she could, trying to hoist him up. "You're not! I didn't - please don't."

Under the light of the bridge, his face was different. There might have been surprise, or tears in his eyes, but she couldn't tell in her wild terror.

And Phaira couldn't help but think of how strange it was that Theron's mouth didn't make that O-shape, not like Nican, or Kadise, or others who fell at her touch.

Maybe because he let go of her hand and held her gaze until he hit the water.

He was gone. He was dead.

They were all dead.

This isn't supposed to happen. It isn't supposed to just be over.

Her face was tearing apart. Her veins were going to explode.

Too much. Too loud. Too much.

Phaira climbed over the railing, bracing herself against the metal infrastructure. Her toes teetered over the edge. She closed her eyes, wishing with all her might that someone would push, but no, she had to take the leap.

It was time. Finally.

She let the weight of her body move forward. Felt the shift in balance.

The open air. The cool wind.

A hand around her forearm, yanking so hard it made her slip and land on the railing with her already-bruised ribs. As she gasped with pain, that hand continued to yank, sliding her off the railing and onto the asphalt.

Feet thundered past her; ambulance sirens; radio calls for help. Swarms of patrol officers, storming the bridge, leaping on the remaining Savas, chopping and kicking, and knocking the Savas in black to the ground.

And Renzo, collapsing next to her. His eyes were wide and white, and she could make out the sound of his teeth chattering.

Somehow, his arms were around her, and she was clinging to his unfamiliar, bony body, holding onto him like he was a buoy in the ocean, as the fighting continued all around them.

VI.

Phaira refused a memorial service. Not because she didn't love Cohen, of course, or didn't want to honor him, but because she wasn't ready to acknowledge that things had changed. Not yet. Not while Sydel was still asleep.

In West Lea Hospital, Phaira sat on the bedside, and stared at Sydel's thin face. What was going on in that mind? Should she put Sydel out of her misery, if in fact, she was in misery? The doctors were still trying to pinpoint what exactly was wrong with her, asking Phaira and Renzo question after question about her medical history, what exactly had happened on the Lea Bridge when she collapsed. They didn't ask about Cohen, of course. There were no more questions to be asked about her little brother, somewhere in the basement of this place, held in the morgue.

Renzo sat on the other side of the bed. His shoulders were so hunched, his clavicles stuck out from his shirt collar. He hadn't said a word to Phaira since they left the bridge in the ambulance, with Sydel hooked up to machines, Phaira being treated for a cracked rib, lacerations, and a bruised ankle. Cohen was in another ambulance, enclosed in an extra-large body bag. Renzo had thrown up at the sight, and Phaira had to refuse the convulsions that threatened to take over her body. It meant that the pain bloomed in her chest instead, like a stain spreading, and pulsing, and threatening to suffocate.

Cohen wanted to be a hero. More than anything. He wanted to protect us all. We couldn't stop him. It didn't matter if I ran, if I told him no. He had his own ideas for his life.

"Miss Phaira. Mr. Renzo."

Both turned at the sound of the man's voice. Then Phaira sprang to her feet, immediately gasping with pain. She held onto her ribs and remembered how quickly Sydel had healed her ribs in Kings Canyon with just a touch.

"Dr. Sabik," Phaira said, trying to muster a smile, but unable to find the muscles to do so. "I can't - what are you doing here?"

As she spoke, she caught Renzo's confused expression in her peripheral vision. No, he'd never met Sabik; he wouldn't know that the doctor was the one who cured Anandi's father Emir of his blood disorder. The last time she saw the doctor, he was running with Anandi and a wheelchair-bound Emir, as Phaira stayed behind to confront the patrol that came to arrest them all. She'd never thought to look him up, to see if he survived, if he continued his practice elsewhere.

"I came to see Anandi."

Phaira winced again, this time from shame. She didn't realize that Anandi was in the same hospital. How strange, that they were all together.

Not everyone, her mind reminded her. *They haven't found Theron's body yet.*

"How is she?" Phaira asked, pushing down her guilt.

"She has a lot of healing to do," Dr. Sabik took off his glasses and cleaned the lenses as he spoke. "It will be difficult, but she has a solid chance of pulling through."

Doctor speak, Phaira thought. *Nothing definitive.*

"This is your friend, yes?" Sabik asked, gesturing at the bed. "Emir told me what happened and asked me to come and look at her. With your permission, of course."

A spark of hope, somewhere in her brain. If anyone could figure out what was wrong with Sydel, and figure out a way to save her, Sabik could. Look what he had done with Emir and his blood disorder. It was possible. Maybe something was possible.

Phaira glanced at Renzo, wondering if he might argue. Renzo just shrugged, hobbling to the corner of the room.

"Yes," Phaira said. "Of course."

Dr. Sabik studied the medical records and charts provided. He consulted with the doctors and nurses on staff. Then he performed a series of neurological tests, shining light into Sydel's eyes, checking brain waves and reflexes. He nodded to himself as he reviewed the scans and X-rays.

Then he turned back to Phaira. She braced herself for the worst.

"I have ideas."

Phaira felt the air leave her body.

"Ideas," Sabik emphasized, holding up a finger. "I have no definitive answer for why she is not waking up. But I have some ideas for treatment, perhaps a way to stimulate repair to the brain damage, reverse the clotting disorder, and bring her back to consciousness."

Would Sydel even want to wake up? Phaira wondered. *Would she want to be a live without Cohen? What will I say if she comes back? What will I possibly say?*

"There's a complication, however, before I can treat her for anything." Sabik held Phaira's gaze. "There's a possibility that she's pregnant."

Phaira's mouth dropped open. She heard Renzo get to his feet behind her. "That - no, that can't be," she sputtered.

"I'll know for certain in the next few days," Sabik said, gesturing at the medical records. "But if she is with child, I need to know if that's a priority."

"A priority," Phaira repeated, feeling stupid.

"If Miss Sydel would want to delay treatment until the baby is born," Sabik explained gently. "What I have in mind, it could affect the pregnancy."

I didn't even think that they were sleeping together. Phaira let out a weak laugh. *I'm so blind.*

"What, so she's an incubator for months?" Renzo interrupted, his voice gruff. "She just stays in a coma and grows a human?"

"If that is the decision, we'll take the baby as soon as it's viable," Sabik said. "If she holds onto the pregnancy. Then I can begin to treat Sydel."

Phaira couldn't even fathom the idea. *Did she and Cohen plan this? He would have been a great father, better than the* rest of us by far.

This isn't right. How can this be happening?

"Miss Phaira? What would you like me to do?"

"I don't know," Phaira finally managed. "I don't know what to think. I can't make that decision for her. Neither of us can."

She sank heavily down on the bed, staring into Sydel's face. *Wake up*, she demanded. *Wake up and tell me what to do.*

"I understand how difficult this information is...." Sabik tried.

"You don't know about difficult information, whoever you are," Renzo snapped.

"Ren," Phaira warned. "Stop."

She looked down at Sydel again. "Where would the treatment take place? Here?"

"I'm afraid not," Sabik said, lowering his voice. "Any treatment I attempt must take place outside of a hospital. To avoid complications."

"So where, then? Where do you work out of?" Renzo pressed

"At this time, I have no base of operations," Sabik admitted. "And I would need financial assistance to set up my team, and my treatment options. Do you have any funds to support the cost of this endeavor?"

Phaira deflated again. "No. We don't have much of anything anymore."

An idea occurred to her. "But I could get some rana."

She glanced at Renzo, anticipating his protest.

But he just stared at the floor.

So Phaira turned back to Sabik. "If you'll take her on as a patient, I'll get you paid. I swear it. When can you start?"

"As soon as we have a place to go, I'm yours, Miss Phaira."

* * *

"Are you in a lot of pain?" It seemed like a dumb question, but it was the only one that Phaira could think to ask, as she gingerly sat on the edge of the hospital bed.

"It's pretty much the worst thing ever." Anandi's voice was muffled but had that ring of slyness that Phaira remembered. She was still covered with bandages, some showing an orange, oily sheen.

"I'm so sorry this happened," Phaira said. "And that I haven't come to see you." She looked at Anandi's left hand, which was mostly unblemished, and wondered if she should take it, if that was the proper gesture. What did she do when Renzo was hospitalized? She couldn't remember.

"Don't apologize," Anandi said, shifting in her bed. "I should be the one apologizing. I shouldn't have been so petty. If I had been better - "

"I was pretty terrible, too," Phaira pointed out. "I should have listened to what you had to say."

A long silence followed. Through the bandages, Anandi's eyes were rimmed with pink, but sharp, looking Phaira up and down. She had a thousand questions, Phaira could see it. What could she say, really? Even describing the events that took place, it seemed too simple; there wasn't enough weight to express the reality of what she remembered, of what she grieved, and hated herself for grieving.

A tiny, almost unperceivable click in the room.

Phaira's heart leapt.

She got to her feet, swiveling in place and looking for some kind of surveillance. "Who has been here?" she demanded.

But Anandi's gaze was fixed across the room, where a pair of scorched boots lay in the corner. "I heard it too," she whispered. "In my right boot. Hidden compartment."

Phaira crouched down to feel the edges of Anandi's burned boot. Ash smeared across her palm as she searched. There it was, she felt the familiar edges.

She studied the Lissome. It hadn't cracked, and it didn't look like the fire had damaged it.

She held it between thumb and forefinger, and raised it to Anandi's eyeline. "Is this yours?"

Anandi struggled to sit up in the bed. "Give it to me." Her voice was strangely urgent. "Put it on my thigh."

Confused, Phaira placed it on the girl's left thigh, over the scratchy hospital blanket. Balancing the Lissome there, Anandi managed to shift her torso upright. Her heavily bandaged arms on either side of her thigh, she activated the Lissome with a wave of her finger.

The device projected three screens instantly. The pixels highlighted Anandi's shocked face.

"What is it?" Phaira asked. She found her reading glasses and slipped them on, peering over Anandi's shoulders. A financial catalogue, she quickly realized: bank account numbers, routing numbers, business transactions, real estate deeds. She caught names in the scrolling screens. Sava. Sava. Sava. And not just Savas, but the name Ajyo, too. Anandi and Emir were listed, and someone who might have been Anandi's grandmother?

"Why would he do this?" Anandi was whispering. "Why would he give this to me?"

"Who gave this to you?"

But Phaira knew the answer before Anandi said the name.

"Theron told me to hold onto this, that it would unlock eventually," Anandi continued under her breath. "But what am I supposed to do with all this?"

The answer was instantaneous: *Dissolve the accounts. Destroy their resources, their real estate, their dummy bank accounts. It's the only way to decimate syndicate power over Osha.*

And by the look on Anandi's face, she'd come to the same conclusion, staring at Phaira with wonder. "My grandmother's accounts are in here. My father's inheritance."

Phaira tried to process everything, tried to get her tongue to work, even as she wanted to sink into the floor. "Why is your family included in all of this?"

"Because we are connected," Anandi said softly. "Ajyos and Savas. We feed into their activities, whether we are willing or not. So: one stroke to finish it all. It's brilliant, really."

"You don't have to do anything," Phaira told her. "You can think about it. Make sure it's the right thing to do."

Anandi shook her head. "I don't have to think about it."

For the next few minutes, the room was heavy with clicks, swishing screens, error commands, and Anandi's strained breath. Phaira did her best not to pace, not to run her hands through her hair again and again, or let her knees achieve the weakness they wanted. Her thoughts were slotting together, and she was afraid to believe the picture forming in her head: Theron always planned to dismantle the syndicate. He'd been collecting all the financial information for weeks. But he knew he was slated to die, and he wanted to be sure that someone would make the final blow, even if he wasn't around.

But what about all the anti-NINE technology? What about her brother? What about nearly shooting Sydel on the bridge? Was it all a trick? A performance? Was it to propel her to react, to give him a proper death, so he couldn't be seen as a martyr?

"It's done."

The pixelated screens sucked back into the Lissome, and Anandi leaned back with a sigh. To Phaira's surprise, she was smiling. "Well, my family is officially broke. And so is every Sava in Osha."

They're free, she realized. *For the first time, they're free from the Savas.*

And so am I.

VII.

Renzo had gone back to the *Arazura* to sleep, and Phaira was glad for it; it was too awkward to have him in the same space. That evening, Phaira did her best to trim Sydel's fingernails. She didn't want the nurses touching her, as clumsy as Phaira was at anything like caregiving. It was only when she was alone with Sydel that she let tears fall for Cohen, and let the pain sear through her chest. In response, Sydel sighed sometimes, and her fingertips fluttered.

"Phaira."

Her name travelled across the room. Phaira froze, holding the pair of scissors.

"Will she recover?"

Phaira closed the scissors, gripping them in her fist, so the inch of sharpness was exposed

Only then did she twist at the waist to look.

CaLarca wasn't alone in the doorway; she was with her partner, Ganasan, who held their sleeping child against his shoulder. There was a quiet strength to the threesome, and a calmness that Phaira could not recall ever seeing in the woman with the braids. It enraged her. *What do you want now?* she wanted to scream at them. *Haven't you done enough, hurt enough? Are you glad that Cohen is dead? Why do you get a happy ending, and we don't?*

"I don't know," Phaira finally said, her voice tight. "I don't know if she'll wake up."

She looked at the shears clenched in her fists. Then she put them on the bedside table, exhausted to the bone.

"She's pregnant, apparently," she announced, surprised at the confession.

CaLarca's gaze shifted to where the girl lay. "She is. I can see the life." There was both wonder and sorrow in the observation. Phaira saw Ganasan put a hand around CaLarca, how his fingers pressed into her shoulder, and burned desperately for that kind of comfort.

"Can I speak to CaLarca alone?" she asked.

CaLarca and Ganasan exchanged intimate looks.

Then Ganasan ducked out of the room with their son and closed the door.

The three women in the room were silent.

"May I sit?" CaLarca asked, gentleness in the request. It made Phaira want to flinch with suspicion.

But she was so tired of fighting.

Phaira nodded at the bed. "Go ahead."

CaLarca settled onto the mattress, moving stiffly. She was in pain, injured from the fight on the bridge, Phaira realized. What had happened there?

"You shape-shifted." Phaira winced at the term, but it was the only word she could come up with. "You figured out how to change your face, like Kuri did."

"Yes," CaLarca said. "That man was Zarek Voss. One of the original NINE. He betrayed me, so it seemed only right to use his face to betray Joran."

"Where is this Voss now?"

CaLarca's silence gave the answer.

"And you disappeared. How did you do that?"

"Another Nadi trick," CaLarca said. "One I don't want to use again."

She gazed at the girl in the bed, laying her hand over Sydel's. "What are your plans, Phaira? She can't stay here."

"I'm setting up care for her. And treatment. At least, I will when I get the rana."

It was CaLarca's turn to wince. "I put the rana back into your account. Earlier today. It was just a means to.... it was wrong, and I apologize for stealing it. For everything."

"Thank you, I suppose," Phaira said wryly. "But it won't be enough." She glanced at Sydel again. "I'll make up the remainder through jobs on the LRP network."

CaLarca's face showed a hint of a smile. "You will do well, I think, in that role."

"If it makes the rana, then it's worth it," Phaira said with a sigh. "But it's also travelling across Osha, and I can't leave her alone. Emir will be busy with Anandi's recovery, I can't bother him with it. And Renzo...."

Phaira trailed off, looking at her hands. "Plus, this treatment could take months. I need to figure out a secure location to make sure no one interferes."

"I will care for her."

Phaira held her breath.

"And care for the baby, if it is born," CaLarca continued. "Until Sydel wakes up again."

Phaira stared at CaLarca with horror. What manipulation was this?

"No." Phaira felt the word burst out of her mouth. "You have no right. You have no right to even ask for such a thing," she continued to hiss, feeling hot tears coming to her eyes.

"I promise you, Phaira," CaLarca said, her voice husky with grief. "I will guard her with my life. For both of their lives. Ganasan will agree. It's what we are meant to do, what we should have done from the start, when Sydel was a baby. It's only fitting that we care for her offspring too, as needed."

Her eyes were sincere. "You say you need a secure location. Bring her to the South, to our land. We can rebuild to accommodate Sydel's needs, both for comfort and security. We will isolate ourselves for her, to keep her safe. And you would make the final decisions on her care. I would carry out whatever you asked.

"Without arguing with me?" Phaira couldn't help but add.

CaLarca's black eyes glittered. "Perhaps a strong suggestion."

Both women smirked at each other, and Phaira wondered if this was all a dream, including the question that followed: "I have a favor to ask."

CaLarca's eyebrows lifted high.

"I need to develop my Eko," Phaira said. "Just receiving messages isn't enough. I've always been afraid to see what else I could do. Physicality has been the only thing for so long. I don't want to rely on only that anymore. Not if I'm going into LRP work."

CaLarca regarded her with curiosity. "I can show you. If you're certain that's what you want."

"I do." Phaira glanced down at Sydel in the bed.

Because I'm a NINE, whether I like it or not.

And I'm going to use it for good, like she wanted.

* * *

As the sun rose over West Lea Hospital, Phaira and Renzo sat in the *Arazura* cockpit. Every part of the ship was empty, and echoing. Phaira's chest ached, straining for the sound of her little brother's chortle, or heavy footsteps. She could smell him. She could feel him in these walls, and Theron too, somehow. Ghosts in these walls were stretching out to touch her. She hunched her shoulders and drew her knees to her chest, feeling the sheathed katana press against her back.

Renzo was the one to break the silence. "I'm going back to work."

"What do you mean? At the university?"

"The anti-NINE tech business is valid," Renzo muttered, gazing out the windshield. "And needed. I can rebuild, and keep developing - "

"It's a Sava business," Phaira said, curling her lip with disgust. "You can't be serious."

"It's my company," Renzo corrected. "It's in my name. Doesn't matter how it started, it can continue as a legitimate manufacturing company."

"After everything that's happened, that's what you want to do? Make weapons?"

"It's needed," Renzo shot back. "Whether you want to admit it or not. There's more NINE out there. And some may try and hurt people."

In the silence that followed, a chasm loomed between them, so deep and hollow that Phaira could feel the reverberations. What would they be without Cohen to connect them? Maybe this was the last time they would speak to each other, without that common thread. Her chest wrenched with pain, and she had to steel her eyes, her throat, to keep tears from being seen or heard. He seemed even colder than before, even more shut off and hardened. Maybe she looked the same to him.

"You're joining LRP?" he asked gruffly, not looking at her.

"I am."

"I can give you some equipment. In case you run into a NINE."

Phaira thought about arguing, but she was too sad to try. "I'll think about it," she finally responded.

"And we have to do something for him," Renzo added. "Before we - he deserves it."

"I know," Phaira admitted. "I know."

They never did talk about final arrangements, the three of them. What would Cohen want? Where would he want to be laid to rest? The terminology, the thought, made Phaira want to put her fist through the *Arazura* windshield. Instead she dug her fingernails into her palms, and felt the pain, and felt guilty for feeling anything at all.

"Maybe a plaque next to Father. On the bridge." There was a choke to Renzo's voice.

"Toomba," Phaira finally spoke. "He'd want to go back to the mountains. He was going to go back, anyways. I think he felt at home there."

Renzo nodded, staring at his hands.

The *Arazura* console flashed; a call through the soundsystem. Renzo leaned forward to connect.

"Officer Lore?"

Renzo's eyebrows shot up his forehead. *What?* he mouthed.

Phaira flapped her hand at the speaker. "Phaira is fine," she said loudly. "What is it?"

"I'm outside. Got a minute?"

Phaira met Renzo's eyes. He dropped his gaze and fiddled with the console. There was nothing more she could think to say to Renzo, in that moment, anyways.

On the way out, she stopped into her cabin.

Then, clomping down the unfolded stairs, Phaira held out the folded uniform, the badge, and the Compact to Ozias, who waited on the ground below.

"Here," she said, shoving them at the detective. "I'm not patrol. So take them back."

Ozias held the bundle and the weaponry for a long pause, an annoyed look on her face. Then, to Phaira's surprise, she shoved the contents back at her. "You are, and I have a case for you."

"Did you not just hear me?" Phaira hissed. She pushed the bundle back at Ozias. "I'm joining the LRP network. It's a better fit for me, anyways. I'm no officer. I appreciate all you did, but - "

"You're not the least bit curious about the assignment?"

Phaira pressed her lips together, air ballooning at the back of her throat. "No, I'm not curious," she finally responded. "Nor available. I need rana now."

"For your brother's burial?"

Phaira flinched. Then she forced her mouth to work. "Yes. And other things."

Ozias regarded her with a curious expression. "Thought you'd want to know that we've closed the case file on Theron."

It took effort to push the words out: "You found him?"

"Not yet."

Her hopes sprung. Did he fake all this to escape, finally? Could he have survived the fall from the bridge? Was it all an elaborate plot?

"But the river is high, so it could take a while to recover the body," Ozias added. "Either way, with the family gone, we can close the files on the Sava Syndicate, and leave them in history where they belong."

To Phaira's surprise, Ozias's expression grew thoughtful, her bottom lip bitten. "I've been following that syndicate for ten years. It's strange to think that it's gone, just like that. Of course, one will rise to take its place, eventually. It's just a matter of time. I will never lack for work. And neither will you, if you'll keep working for me."

"I told you, I'm not an officer."

"Then don't be official patrol. It works, anyways, for an unofficial investigation."

"What do you mean?"

"There's a new initiative to reopen unsolved case files across Osha, specifically ones involving strange behavior, or unexplainable deaths, to see if they are NINE-related. Hundreds of cases, potentially, to investigate. They might even move me up a rank to supervise it."

"Congratulations, I guess," Phaira said sourly. "What do you need me for?"

"I would feel better having someone with some expertise at the forefront, especially in the more difficult areas to access. As you say, you're no officer. But this is no standard patrol investigation. I need someone who can move outside the rules as needed and take care of themselves on their own. And be discreet, of course."

Phaira didn't know what to say, other than to repeat gruffly: "I need rana now."

"If cleared, I'll have discretionary funds," Ozias said. "I can advance you a certain amount. And you can still join the LRP network, I know you're already registered. But I ask that, if I call, you make my case the priority."

She nodded at the bundle in Phaira's hands, which she realized was still there, weighing down her arms. "You can think about it. For now, keep the Compact, and the uniform. Whether you agree to work for me or not, they might come in handy."

Ozias turned away. "I'll be in touch. Settle your affairs. Because I'm going to need you very soon."

* * *

When the parcel was placed in Phaira's arms, she felt the hard ridges within.

"What is this?" she asked Emir, who bore the package.

"Your Calises," Anandi said from her bed. Her bandages had been freshly changed, and there was a little more life in her eyes and voice. "And your Ikani Mala passport."

Phaira jerked her chin back. "You've had them all this time?"

"You asked me to keep them safe in Liera. I just never had a chance to give them back to you."

Then Anandi frowned. "Well? Aren't you going to open your present?"

Phaira stared at the buddle. "I - I don't know. If I want them back."

Anandi frowned. "I thought you loved these things. You wanted to go back to my grandmother's house for them in Honorwell."

That made Phaira think of Theron. She neatly sidestepped the memory. "I do. I did. But they're - not right."

Anandi's face screwed up; she clearly didn't understand. Phaira opened her mouth to try and explain herself, but then pressed her lips together. She didn't want to get into the fact that the Calises not only reminded her of life in the military, but of all the mistakes she'd made. The pistols were exclusive, and complicated, and an ego boost to wield, but they weren't practical, not for the line of work that Phaira was going into.

"I'll keep them," she told Anandi. "Thank you."

Unsaid, she made a vow: *I'll keep them to remember who I was, and what I no longer am.*

"You'll be safe, right?" Phaira couldn't help but ask. "Without me here?"

"You sure can make a girl blush, Phaira," Anandi said with a tired smile. "Paranoid and protective as always. But I don't have much of a choice.

Then her smile faded. "How can you trust CaLarca to not hurt Sydel? I mean - after everything she's done? What if she - ?"

"We have a common goal," Phaira interrupted gently. "I believe her, and her intentions. For the first time, I really do."

Anandi gave a big huff of annoyance. "I really don't understand you people. And I think I'm going to stop trying."

"Ani," Emir chided gently.

Then he turned to Phaira. "I'll watch the process," Emir confirmed. "Ensure that Sydel arrives safely in the South, and alert you if there's any hint of trouble or deception. In the meantime, Anandi will teach me to create security provisions around the property, ensure a no-fly zone is instilled, and that it stays off any maps. It will be invisible for as long as you want it to be, Phaira, we promise. She'll be safe."

Emir's voice grew tight. "I hope Sabik can help her. I'll be praying that he does, every day. And if I can help, somehow..."

Impulsively, Phaira reached out and hugged Emir tight around the shoulders. From the tiny squawk he let out, the man wasn't expecting the physicality, and Phaira felt awkward immediately, but she held on anyways.

"Oh sure, he gets a hug," she heard Anandi complain.

Phaira smiled against Emir's shoulder, and again when she felt the light pat on her back, a comforting pat, followed by a light rub.

* * *

Phaira dreamt of the bridge. She felt the whistle of air, and the hard smack of water. She struggled to keep her mouth at the water's surface, even as it poured down her throat, and her lungs threatened to explode, and water came out of her eyes and mouth and ears.

When she woke in her cabin, the transfer process had begun. Thanks to Anandi and Emir, Phaira was able to follow Sydel's position remotely from the Arazura, and then from her Lissome, as she and Renzo arrived in the Cyan Mountains, and the town of Toomba. The grandmother, Vyoma, was waiting for them, straight and stocky, unmoving as the mountains. She instructed her militia to remove Cohen's body, housed in a cold storage compartment, from the *Arazura* hanger, and bring it into her house. Renzo and Phaira were glad to stand aside and let the woman take over with her gruff instructions.

Per tradition, Cohen's body was cremated in a deep hole in the mountains. The smoke made Phaira retch and Renzo nearly passed out in her arms.

And when darkness fell, Vyoma bundled straw together, binding it with rope to create limbs, and laying the straw body on a pyre. Cohen's ashes were shaken into the straw, and Vyoma set fire to it, while the residents of Toomba watched.

Smoke bloomed up into the night sky, and Phaira knew that it was over.

At the back of the crowd, one of the militia offered Phaira a grey twisted cigarette: to ease the mind, he told her.

She shook her head, and watched the fire.

Afterwards, Renzo and Phaira had flown into the south territory, to the outskirts of the town where camp had been set up, and construction had already begun on CaLarca's property. Phaira asked to be dropped down from a distance, so she could hike in and observe the security measures. Renzo agreed.

They didn't hug, nor say much other than farewell. Truthfully, it was hard for Phaira to look Renzo in the eye. Then the *Arazura* glimmered blue in the morning light, rose over her head, and barreled away.

One day, Phaira thought as she watched it disappear. *One day we'll talk about it. We'll figure it out.*

As promised, Anandi and Emir had set up an impressive amount of security perimeters; as soon as Phaira stepped foot onto the property, an alarm was tripped, and drones swiveled overhead, and she heard the hum of electric fences an inch from her skin.

Soon, Ganasan came running, full of apologizes, but Phaira waved him off, pleased at the progress. No one would take a step onto the property without being noticed. Just as she wanted.

True to her word, Ozias had forwarded enough rana to get Sabik and his team on their way to the South. And Ozias had already provided the first assignment: reports of domestic violence with a couple in the Mac; strange, unexplainable behavior from the wife of the pairing, seizures, and prophecies that made her husband beat her more. Phaira was to investigate, observe, and depending on circumstances, either neutralize the situation or take the potential NINE into custody.

If this woman was NINE, Ozias warned in her notes, she needed help, and not just from her household. Perhaps there had to be some kind of resource for NINE in Osha. Maybe

Phaira could be the first connection, could help to set up some kind of safe haven.

Phaira chose not to respond in that moment to that inquiry.

Instead, alone in the tent with Sydel, Phaira put the tip of her finger against Sydel's abdomen, wondering if there was a trace of a swell there, or if she was just seeing things.

The girl's skin seemed flusher. She took deeper breaths, like her eyes were about to burst open.

Maybe the child was keeping her alive.

Maybe it would jumpstart her brain.

She pressed her finger into Sydel's abdomen, feeling the hard lump.

A child, in there. Cohen's child.

Phaira bent over Sydel's body, focusing on where her finger pressed.

I'll be back, she whispered in her head. *I'll always come back.*

THE END

Phaira Lore will return in Mobius Loop.

about:

Loren Walker is a Pushcart Prize 2017 nominee; her poems have appeared in QU Journal, the West Texas Literary Review, and River River, as well as the anthologies Routes and Frequency Writers City and Sea. Her debut fiction novel, EKO, won the Library Journal Indie E-book Award for Science Fiction, was awarded a BRAG Medallion, shortlisted for the Half the World Global Literari Award, and selected as a Shelf Unbound 2016 Notable Indie. The sequels, NADI and INSYNN were released in 2017, with the final book of the NINE Series NYX to released in 2018. Originally from Ontario, Canada, Loren Walker now works and lives in Rhode Island.

thank you:

to my family and friends, my eternal cheerleaders.
to my beta reader Jill Corley, whose dramatic reactions always make me smile.
to my editor Lindsay Galloway, and to Deranged Doctor Design, for making NYX look good.
and to you, for buying this book.